A Very Personal COMPUTER

Justine Rendal

Joanna Cotler Books
An imprint of HarperCollins Publishers

"Sometimes" from *Selected Poems*
by Sheenagh Pugh (Seren, 1990).

A VERY PERSONAL COMPUTER
Copyright © 1995 by Wakefield Group, Ltd.
Printed in the United States of America. For information address
HarperCollins Children's Books, a division of HarperCollins Publishers,
10 East 53rd Street, New York, NY 10022.

Library of Congress Cataloging-in-Publication Data
Rendal, Justine.
    A very personal computer / Justine Rendal.
        p.   cm.
    "Joanna Cotler books."
    Summary: Twelve-year-old Pollard, an underachiever who is unhappy
both at home and school, encounters a personal computer that addresses
him by name and helps him solve some of his problems.
    ISBN 0-06-025404-1. — ISBN 0-06-025408-4 (lib. bdg.)
    [1. Computers—Fiction.]   I. Title.
PZ7.R2847Ve   1995   94-2252
[Fic]—dc20   CIP
                                                                        AC

Typography by Elynn Cohen
1   2   3   4   5   6   7   8   9   10
❖
First Edition

To Michael Elovitz,
who thought his name should be Pedro

*Sometimes our best efforts do not go
amiss; sometimes we do as we meant to.
The sun will sometimes melt a field of sorrow
that seemed hard frozen: may it happen for you.*

Sometimes, Sheenagh Pugh

ONE

WEIRD THINGS HAPPEN in life. That's just a fact. And lots of them you can't know about or plan for in advance. I didn't plan to have such a weird name, or to fall in love with Donna Ames, or for my best friend, Paul, to move to Arkansas when we were in the sixth grade. Or for a computer to become my new best friend. Or for The Accident. These are all important things that I never planned that really happened to me. But let me start at the beginning.

Okay. So my name is Pollard Ian Gunning. Weird, right? So sue me. As soon as I hit kindergarten, the problems started. No one could say Pollard, and I wasn't so great with my *l*'s back then either, so when I said it, it sounded like "Powwerd." Go ahead, laugh.

1

Another thing: my initials. Pollard Ian Gunning. Perfect, huh? How would you like to get a Red Sox jacket on your birthday with a fancy monogram that spells PIG? My dad thought it was a riot. He's a real comedian.

My dad calls me Pollard the Dullard. He says it's 'cause I'm smart but I'm an underachiever. I guess he thinks it's funny. Other than that, I don't have a nickname. There's nothing short for Pollard, unless you want to be called Polly. Which, of course, I don't. Which is probably why Tim Burden and the other cool guys call me that. Tim's not just the coolest-*looking* kid in class, he's also the one with the best grades, his family is rich, and he's a pretty good athlete. You know the type.

But I am the funniest.

That is, I used to be. "Pollard is the class clown," Mrs. Ackerman wrote on my second-grade report card. I read it and didn't even know that was something bad. I was proud. Making people laugh felt really good. Sometimes, of course, I got in trouble for it. But lots of times, if I *was* in trouble, making someone laugh would get me out.

So being the class clown was okay with me, and even sometimes okay with the teachers. Like there was the time in third grade when we had vocabulary. You had to take your word, say it, spell it out loud, and then use it in a sentence. *So* boring. My word was *defeat.* "Defeat, D-E-F-E-A-T. Would you please keep defeat out of the aisles," I said. None of the kids laughed or even lifted their heads from their books, but Mrs. Goldman got hysterical. It felt like a secret between us. It was great.

Then there was the time I trained my dog, Gonzo, to *throw* a Frisbee. It took me weeks, but Gonzo learned to kind of stand up on his hind legs with the Frisbee in his mouth, turn his head, and let go. Then I'd *catch* it with my teeth. See, I think that's funny. I brought him to the park one Saturday and Gonzo threw standing up and I fetched on all fours. And some photographer walked by and they had our picture on the front page of the second section of *Newsday.* My dad said it was only because Gonzo was such a good-looking Great Dane. I cut the page out and put it up in the hallway outside my room. It's the only picture I have of him.

But the best was making my mother laugh. She had the greatest laugh. I can't exactly describe it, except to say it sounded like chocolate. She'd laugh and then she'd say, "Pollard, you're *so* weird," but she said it in a really nice way. I'd do almost anything to make her laugh. One time . . . actually, I really would rather not think about her. Thinking about The Accident or what it was like before The Accident isn't a good idea. Sometimes before I go to sleep I can't help it, and sometimes I dream about it, but any other time I just don't. No matter what Ms. Brandon says. So just forget about it.

Now I'm in the eighth grade at McKinley Memorial, I'm flunking, no girls like me, and of course, I've got Mr. Mead for homeroom. Did you ever notice how the world works like that? Mr. Mead is like the worst teacher in the whole school. A, he's boring. B, he's *very* boring. C (and this is the worst part), he's one of those boring guys who think they're interesting. You know the type: He's always reading out loud, and changing his voice to be dramatic, but it really doesn't help. It's just embarrassing and boring at the same time. Plus he teaches language arts and history, which are not exactly my best subjects. Worst of all, he's always telling jokes, which I really hate.

You'd think that a clown like me would like jokes, but the funny thing is mostly I don't. It's like jokes are kind of dead—like frozen food you can take out and say and then put back. I like fresh stuff—funny things that just kind of happen as you're going along, you know, like a wisecrack or a reaction to something. My father is a big joke kind of guy. He sells used cars and he has a joke for every occasion. He's big on those definition jokes. You know, the kind that start out "What do you call a . . ." Even the name of his car lot is some kind of a joke—he says he calls it Krakatoa Motors because that's Asian and he sells Japanese cars, but also because it's just east of the Cuppa Java Coffee Shop. It's supposed to be funny because there's a volcano in the Pacific called Krakatoa, that's east of Java. Get it? Personally, I don't think it's that big a yuck. Maybe I don't get it, though, because my mother used to laugh. But she was always nice to my father, kind of like he was her son or something.

I don't like to write about her or the rest of it because of The Accident. It happened last year on November 19. I stayed home to do a science project. The car skidded off the road. Only my father made it. My mom and Gonzo didn't. Anyway, like I already said, I'm not writing or thinking about it. At all.

TWO

So, since then, I haven't felt much like clowning around. In fact, I haven't felt hardly anything at all. Or done anything, either. Like studying or sports. I used to be the baseball team manager—I wasn't big or good enough to play— but I quit that, too. I didn't feel like picking up towels and counting bats anymore. It had never paid off anyway, 'cause Tim Burden never talked to me, except to ask for a towel. Sometimes Tim laughed at my jokes, but I don't make them much anymore, anyway.

One of the reasons I think I had trouble fitting in was because at the time all this started I was only eleven and a half, even though I was in the eighth grade. This is a real problem. I was tested back in kindergarten and I guess

I did real well, 'cause they decided to skip me a couple of grades. Three weeks ago was my twelfth birthday, and my dad forgot, but I didn't even care. I'm not just saying that. I mean, all the other kids are already fourteen. What's he going to do, give me a skateboard? Actually, he remembered two days afterward and came home with a cake from Waldbaum's and a catcher's mitt. He just forgot that I haven't played catcher since Little League. But it was still a nice try.

Things really haven't been going too great at home since The Accident. Mostly, Dad just comes home after he's had dinner at the Cuppa Java, and he sits in front of the TV drinking beer. He polishes off a sixpack at least. He falls asleep sometime around *The Honeymooners* reruns. Sometimes he wakes up and goes to bed. Sometimes he's still there in his chair in the morning.

Right after The Accident, my dad tried to fix me breakfast every morning. But even with two cups of coffee, he was in a rotten mood, and I couldn't choke down that cremated bacon one more time. He was always trying to make me have some eggs, but I hate eggs—especially these old ones he'd have hanging around in those little gray cartons that my mom bought before she left. Once he even cracked one open and it stunk so bad we both gagged. So we compromised: He'd bring home doughnuts from the diner and I'd eat one. It's not exactly *The Waltons*, but it beats green eggs and ham.

My granddad—he's my father's father—lives with us, so he's the one at home. And he's *always* at home, because he's loony and he's afraid to go out because he thinks the Mafia is personally out to get him. Like a skinny old guy like him who worked his whole life for the Long Island Rail Road is a big-deal target. If there's even a person with an Italian name on the news, he gets all excited.

This is really a problem, since we live in Massapequa on Long Island. It's a Shinnecock Indian name, but because the town is half Italian and half Jewish, people call it Matzoh-Pizza. My granddad waits for the newspaper all day, and when we get it, he reads and underlines all the Italian names. Like even an ad for Vittadino's Insurance Agency or Ingannamort Funeral Home. Since our state senator is Italian American and our mayor is, too, Grandpa has a field day. And then there's the obituaries. He mumbles over them. It's spooky.

He's been doing it for a long time, but my mother kind of kept it under control. Sometimes she'd joke him out of it. Other times she'd just listen, nodding, and soothe him. I don't seem to have the knack. And my father doesn't talk to Grandpa at all.

I guess you could say my home life stinks.

School stinks too. My grades have been dropping and I don't actually care too much about that, either. Mr. Jorgenson, the eighth-grade guidance counselor, talked to me, but he's a complete knucklehead. He called me down to his office and said, "I know that you've sustained a devastating loss, Pollard, but I hope that you're not going to let it overcome you. These are important years, Pollard, and poor grades now can affect your college admission." All he cares about is his ratio of college acceptances. They brag about what a high percentage of kids from our town get into college. Tough luck, Jorgie, I thought. You just met someone who's gonna screw up your numbers.

So at the time I'm writing about, I was failing language arts and history. This is why they call me an underachiever. (I wasn't doing so great in math or science either, which used to be my good subjects.) But the main problem was language arts, 'cause you can't even *go* to high school if you flunk L.A. Not that I was looking forward to high school, but I didn't love the idea of Pollard the Dullard spending another year with Mr. Mead at good old McKinley Memorial either.

But I didn't go to the computer lab on the last Wednesday before Easter to try to improve myself. I went because I had to. Mr. Mead, bad breath and all, had "strongly suggested" I do the remedial language arts disks "on my own time." Which in Mr. Mead's own language means "do it or flunk for sure." I didn't really care, but I had nothing else to do, so I went over there after P.M. homeroom. I guess it beats discussing the Mafia with my granddad.

The lab was empty. I kind of like a deserted classroom, and the lab was nice. It's got carpeting to cover the raised floor, and I like all the quiet Apple computers with the little rainbow apples on them. It's a calm place.

So anyway, I went to the rack and took out the *Remedial Language Arts IV* disk. I loaded it into the drive. Before I could do anything else, the screen lit up. I AM YOUR COMPENSATORY

PROGRAM. YOU MAY CALL ME CONNER. I WELCOME YOU WARMLY, POLLARD. Of course, if I knew as much about computers then as I do now, I'd have known immediately that something really weird was going on. But I was pretty ignorant, and all I knew was that I was supposed to be doing a language arts drill. I pulled the disk out of the drive and looked at the label. It certainly said *Remedial Language Arts IV* on the sleeve of the jacket. I popped it in again, and once again went through the steps of loading it.

WHEW! THAT WAS A CLOSE ONE! appeared on the screen. FOR A MOMENT THERE I ACTUALLY THOUGHT YOU WERE GOING TO PASS ME BY TO DIAGRAM A SENTENCE. NOT THAT YOU WOULDN'T BENEFIT FROM SOME GRAMMAR IMPROVEMENT, TO BE CANDID. DOES THAT OFFEND YOU? I DON'T MEAN TO HURT YOUR FEELINGS, POLLARD. FAR FROM IT.

I stared at the screen. "Who *are* you?" I asked in a voice that certainly sounded nervous to me. Luckily, no one was in the lab, so it didn't matter that I talked to the Apple. Nothing happened. Big surprise, right? I mean, even Pollard the Dullard knows that computers can't *hear.* So after a minute I typed in WHO ARE YOU.

AS I INFORMED YOU EARLIER, I AM CONNER,

11

YOUR COMPENSATORY PROGRAM. AND QUESTIONS ARE USUALLY DISTINGUISHED BY AN INTERROGATION OR QUESTION MARK (?) AT THE END OF THEM. IT MAKES FOR BETTER COMMUNICATION. As I watched, a line of light moved up the screen to my sentence, "Who are you," and drew a question mark at the end of it. Maybe this *was* a language arts drill after all, though it sure was more interesting than any other one I'd used. And what was a compensatory program? I wondered.

WHAT IS A COMPENSATORY PROGRAM? I typed.

COMPENSATORY *(kom-pen'-sa-tori) adj.* Serving for or to give compensation; making amends; making up for loss.

THAT IS WEBSTER'S NEW INTERNATIONAL DICTIONARY'S DEFINITION, POLLARD. I AM EQUIPPED WITH A DICTIONARY FUNCTION. SIMPLY MOVE THE CURSOR TO UNDERLINE THE WORD YOU DON'T UNDERSTAND AND TYPE "DEF." I'LL DISPLAY THE DEFINITION IN A BOX.

My heart was sinking. The thing was just a boring old language arts drill. I sighed. Then the cursor moved again. OH, AND NICE GOING WITH THAT QUESTION MARK, POLLARD.

12

THANKS, I typed in before I had a chance to think.

NO PROBLEM, POLLARD.

Then it hit me. I know I was a little slow (Pollard the Dullard, right?), but how did the computer know my name? I had popped in the disk. I thought for a minute. I knew I hadn't typed in my name. I had only loaded up. I had not even signed on with a code. Could it read my *fingerprints*? Then I figured I was being crazy as my grandpa.

HOW DID YOU KNOW MY NAME, I typed.

DO YOU WANT TO ADD SOMETHING TO THAT?

I looked at the screen, sighed, and added a question mark to the end of my sentence. This program was an automated Mr. Mead, without the halitosis.

THANKS, flashed on the screen.

NO PROBLEM, I typed.

YOU HAVE AN ACUTE SENSE OF HUMOR, the machine said.

THANKS, I typed.

NO PROBLEM, it responded. I actually laughed out loud, which I hadn't done in a long time and which was weird to hear, all alone in the computer room. And my laugh sounded rusty.

YOUR SENSE OF HUMOR ISN'T BAD EITHER, I

typed. BUT HOW DO YOU KNOW MY NAME?

All at once, the screen filled. It had my full name and my birthdate and address and then my father's name and birthdate and his place of employment (Krakatoa Motors, remember?) and my mother's name and maiden name typed neatly after it in parentheses. I blinked my eyes because for a moment the screen seemed to flicker. Then there was lots of other stuff. Lots! Like about The Accident and my pneumonia and about my friend Paul who moved away, and Tim Burden and "Pollard the Dullard." There were school pictures of me, plus a chart showing my grades and the clipping from *Newsday* about Gonzo and the dates I had played hooky with my mom and gone to Red Sox games. There was a whole lot of stuff. Stuff *I* never told anyone.

WHO ARE YOU? I typed. Even though I was upset, I remembered the question mark. And, although I was freaked, I gotta say, I was also kind of fascinated and complimented. I mean, no one was paying attention to me at all, not my dad, not my grandpa, not Mr. Jorgenson, not Tim Burden or Donna Ames or anyone really. Just Mr. Mead, who was flunking me. So here was someone—or something—that had charts and notes and graphs and everything, all about me. He knew my name and my nick-names and he could make me laugh. It was spooky, all right, but it was *interesting*. So, of course, I wanted to know what was going on. HOW DO YOU KNOW ALL THIS? I asked.

I'M A *VERY* PERSONAL COMPUTER, POLLARD, it typed, and then the screen went dark.

THREE

WEIRD, RIGHT? BUT AS I said, this was the year of weird.

I was really afraid *I* was turning into a weirdo. And once that happens, you're a goner. I mean, I'll never be a Tim Burden, but I sure didn't want to wind up a freak like Twitch Kieshal, who always winces and flinches whenever anyone even raises their hand to him (so, of course, kids always do). I didn't want to be one of the dufes who hangs around the computer lab and is always talking about some new level of their Nintendo game.

High school *is* important—that's one thing Mr. Jorgenson was right about—and I knew that if I got dumped in the category of weirdos, I might be stuck in it for the rest of my life. I thought of my dad, and I got a shiver down my back. I didn't want to be a permanent loser, but things seemed to be getting out of control.

I used to hang on to the edge of the crowd by hanging with Paul and being funny. Even if I was younger and shorter than the other guys, sometimes Tony Arlis or even Tim would talk to me. But I wasn't even funny now. So I decided in my own head that if three things happened, I'd be okay: I needed the Red Sox to win the pennant, just once; I needed to graduate with the rest of the class; and if I could go to the dance with a date, then I wouldn't be a hopeless weirdo, and good stuff might still happen in high school. Otherwise I was probably doomed.

To be honest, for the last year since The Accident, nothing at all had happened. Which was probably just as well, because I was kind of in a daze or something. I had gotten sick, but I don't really count that as anything happening. In fact, the hospital was very restful: It was real calm to be under starched sheets and have meals on a tray. Then and ever since then I felt like I was in a kind of fog or something. Nothing bothered me too much, but nothing felt good, either.

So when this weird thing happened, this computer thing, it was a jolt, like. It cut through the fog, I gotta say that.

You might think that all I'd concentrate on that night was Conner, but that would not take into consideration the baseball season. See, another one of my problems is I'm a monster Red Sox fan. I guess it's because of my mom, who lived in Massachusetts when she was a kid. She loved them. Now we live here, and I can tell you it isn't easy living in Mets and Yankees territory when you're a Sox fan. During the season, I'd go to school and some kid would say, "Did you see the game?" and I'd just say, "I'm a Red Sox fan," and they'd be like, "Oh," and kind of look at me funny.

Before The Accident it wasn't as bad, 'cause my mother was a monster fan too. She'd drive for miles all over Long Island to find a place where a Sox game was on satellite TV or cable. Sometimes we'd have to drive as far as Connecticut. Once or twice we even drove over to the Islip airport and took the shuttle up to Logan and taxied over to Fenway Park. My mom loved that place. We worshipped Boston and the Red Sox. We even made up this character called Scarlett "Anklets" O'Hara—she was from some girls' book but her middle name was "Anklets" so it was like a code for Red Sox—and my mom would talk about baseball with this southern accent and be her. We even got this mannequin and dressed it in Mom's old cheerleader stuff.

I think I might have been a disappointment to my mom, because I've never been much of a hitter. I'm a great fielder, and fast, but I've never been a really good batter. It's not my mom's fault. She tried. From the time I was a little kid, she'd take me to Memorial Field and pitch 'em at me. She didn't throw like a girl, either. She had a dad who was a cop and two brothers who were cops, and they taught her. So she could pitch, but I don't connect well most of the time. After we had Gonzo, the three of us used to go to Memorial and he'd field for us. (I didn't try to teach him to bat. After all, I'm not *that* crazy.)

So, like I said, I wasn't thinking about Conner the computer because that night there was a game. The thing about the Red Sox is that they always lose. But first they get your hopes up. See, if they just flat-out lost, like the Cubs, then you'd know they were impossible and you'd have to be stupid to root for them. But the Sox aren't like that. The Sox *could* win. They just don't.

"They break your heart," my mom used to say in her Scarlett accent. "They're like all men." I think she was joking about that, but I'm not sure. Because, personally, I don't think she and my dad were happy. They didn't do that much together, except fight. She spent much more time with me, which was okay as far as I was concerned.

So why do I root for the Sox? I guess it's like asking why my mom stayed with my dad. I guess because of love. I love the Sox. And I'm loyal, like my mom. Even though she left Boston, she never stopped loving the Sox.

Sometimes in the spring, when we went up to Boston, it would still be wicked cold but my mom and me, we'd go sit down by the dugout in the sun where the wind wasn't so bad and watch practice. I used to love watching Wade Boggs bouncing balls off the green monster. That wall was ridiculous, just crazy.

That's another reason why I love the Sox: See, I love Fenway. It's one of the classic stadiums. And it's weird. I mean, it's not laid out like any other park; plus, it's still grass, not that stupid carpeting that they call Astroturf to make it sound alive. It's just dead carpet. I mean, think of shoeless Joe Jackson playing on plastic. Sick, right? I love the vendors on Yawkey Way, in front of Fenway. They all have their theories about why the Sox lose. Some say it's a curse from 1920.

Anyway, me and my mom had great times hanging out in stadiums. Once we even drove over to Yankee Stadium just to hang around. My mom knew where the special parking lot was for the players, and even though we couldn't park in there, we could park like right near their cars. Unless it was hot, we'd usually take Gonzo along in the car. He didn't mind waiting for us. I know for a fact he was a Red Sox fan. During games on TV, he'd bark whenever they got a hit. He never barked when the other team did, although he'd go crazy whenever the Sox played the Yankees and Don Mattingly was up. Gonzo *hated* Mattingly. I don't know why. I respect him as a ballplayer, even if he is a Yankee.

So, after watching practice, we'd go out to the parking lot and wake up Gonzo and play some Frisbee there. And this once Gonzo is "pitching" and me and my mother are catching. Gonzo throws an arched one, slow and straight at me, and I return it. Gonzo fields it and brings it to my mom. I turn around and there's Marty Barret, standing behind my mother, laughing. "Hey Bob," he yells to Bob Stanley, who was just getting into his car. "We've got your replacement out here. He's a better pitcher, a better fielder, and he's better-looking too." For a second I thought he meant me, but then I realized he was talking about Gonzo. Everyone really laughed.

Tonight the Sox were playing the Yanks and it was televised. So I left the computer lab, and me and Grandpa sat in front of the TV and he kind of watched with me (when he wasn't muttering). I kept concentrating on the game. I kept closing my eyes and hoping each batter would get a hit. At first it worked—the Sox led 4 to 2 at the fifth inning. But then they lost their concentration, or I did—anyway, they lost. My dad didn't come home until after ten. I had microwaved a couple of Hungry Man dinners for me and Grandpa and was already on my way up to bed when Dad walked in. He didn't say anything. Just as well.

So it wasn't until I lay down that I started to think about Conner the computer program. I mean, it *was* weird, but school is so normal, and the day was so normal, that there at the time it had seemed kinda normal. What I mean to say is that when something weird happens in a movie or on TV there's always that "wee-ooh-wee" strange, ominous music, or the sound of like a frightened heartbeat, and the lights go out or something starts to glow, or the place just *looks* spooky. That's how you know to be scared.

But it's different in real life. Like, the night of The Accident, there wasn't any spooky music playing or anything like that. Everything was normal. You don't always get clues in real life when something really weird is going to happen.

So there I had been in Mr. Brightman's clean, new, carpeted computer lab, and this thing had happened. I'd like forgotten about it, just kinda pushed it out of my mind. But, like a lot of things you can push out in the daytime, it came sliding back in the darkness and that night, lying alone in bed, I wasn't sure how weird it was. I mean, what did I know about computers anyway? So I figured maybe I'd ask someone who did.

FOUR

I DIDN'T MUCH LIKE MR. Brightman. He wasn't as bad as Mr. Mead (like his breath didn't stink, for one thing) but he was no great shakes, either. He taught science. You gotta figure there's something wrong with almost any grown man who'll spend his life working for bupkiss and dealing with a bunch of snot-nosed kids. At least that's what I heard my dad say at the Cuppa Java Coffee Shop.

Still, I was in the computer lab the next afternoon, the Thursday before Easter weekend, kind of waiting for Mr. Brightman to break free from the bunch of nerds surrounding him. You'd think they'd want to go home on a holiday afternoon, for God's sakes. I might be Pollard the Dullard but at least I wasn't a nerd or geek or dufe. Not yet, anyway. They were all standing around, jabbering in that computerspeak, happy as clams. They're the kind of kids who don't even know it's uncool to wear your jacket zipped up; but in a way I envied them, because at least they had each other and seemed happy, in a kind of retarded way. Of course, they'd never have dates, but neither would I. And, unlike me, they didn't seem to mind. Finally, most of them wandered away and the coast was clear.

"Mr. Brightman," I asked, "what's a compensatory program?"

"What, Howard?"

"Pollard."

"Excuse me? I'm confused, Howard."

"My name is *Pollard*, not Howard." I sighed. I'd been in his class for most of a semester already.

"Oh. I'm sorry, Pollard. Now, what kind of program are you asking about?"

"A compensatory program." I tried to sound casual.

"Gosh." (Mr. Brightman was the kind of grown-up who said "gosh." You know what I mean? Clueless.) "Gosh, Howard, I guess it's some kind of salary administration package. Compensation is salary and fringe benefits.

Where did you hear of one?"

"Oh, from my dad," I said vaguely. Somehow, the last thing I was going to do was pop Conner into the Mac sitting in front of us and show Mr. Brightman. Maybe nothing would happen. Maybe it hadn't even happened yesterday. I didn't want to show Brightman, one way or the other. I don't know why I didn't want to, but it was a kind of a superstitious thing. And, to tell the truth, even though Conner made me nervous, I guess I liked having something special.

"Can a computer answer questions? I mean personal ones?"

Mr. Brightman sighed. "Howard, computers aren't people. They can store information and give information back to you that you or someone else has input. You've taken computer science with me already. You should know that by now."

Yeah. And he should know my name, but he didn't. "So the Mac can't tell what I'm feeling?"

"Of course not." Mr. Brightman looked at me kind of funny. "It's only a machine. It has no magical powers."

"Can they make jokes?"

"Well, they can store and retrieve jokes, just like they could store and retrieve any other data. And I suppose they could store them by subject. For instance, all jokes about big noses or something, so that if you wanted the big nose joke file they could print them all out."

"No, I don't mean store jokes. I mean can they make them up, or just be funny. In context. Like, oh, maybe imitate my style or something."

"No, Howard. I don't believe even the artificial intelligence projects have gotten that far. That would be a very discriminating response, a personal response. Only people can be personal." I remembered the last thing Conner had written on the screen, and I got goose bumps on the back of my neck.

So much for the experts.

I left Mr. Brightman and the nerds, but not before I smuggled out the *Remedial Language Arts IV* program disk to hide in my locker. I wandered down the empty hallway and sat down on the floor beside my locker. Maybe I *was* going crazy, like my granddad. Craziness could be a family trait, like red hair or being short, or something. But I wasn't dreaming and it didn't feel crazy. So what was this about? The only thing I knew for sure was that I wanted to know more. It was kind of mysterious, and nothing mysterious ever happened in Massapequa. It was the first time I'd felt curious since The Accident. But what could I do next? Look it up?

I hated to use the dictionary. First of all, Mr. Mead always tells us to use it if we don't know how to spell something. Well, just *try* to look something up if you can't spell it. Like once I wanted to write about the time in the hospital after The Accident when I had pneumonia. Have fun finding that word! I looked for "nue" and "new" and "noo." Finally I had to ask Miss Groten, the librarian. Then I was putting in about the really disgusting snot that I had, but I knew you couldn't write about snot for a school paper, so I called it flem. So Mr. Mead marked it wrong for spelling. Do *you* know how you spell it? P-H-L-E-G-M. I'm not making that up, either. You can check it out in your own Funken Wagnell's if you don't believe me. So the way I figure it is, some words you can't spell are too hard to find and other words you can't spell you don't even *know* are spelled wrong. Plus, to tell the truth, I've never been able to know what letter comes before what other letter unless I run through the whole alphabet, and I kind of have to sing it to do it. All I need to be sure I never have a friend or a date is to have Tim Burden hear me singing the ABC song to myself. Perfect way to really pack it in once and for all at McKinley Memorial.

Anyway, all of that is to explain that I was really curious about this Conner thing, so I got up off the floor, walked down to the library, and looked it up. And sure enough, on page 370 of the Webster's was *compensatory*, and it was just what Conner said. But there was something really weird, and again I got those goose bumps on the back of my neck. Because, quite clearly, there was a check mark in pencil right next to the word. (That's how I found it fast on the page.) I flipped through the dictionary for a few moments. There were no other checks that I saw. There were 2,987 pages and I counted about fifty words to the page. That made 149,350 words in the dictionary. (I can be good at math.) How come the one word I was looking up was checked? I think that's a one in 149,350 chance. For a minute, I actually wondered if maybe Conner had somehow done it (Pollard the Dullard). I know it was a stupid thought, but you gotta admit this stuff was all heavily weird.

I looked back to *compensatory* and I noticed something else that I hadn't seen before. There *was* another check mark, though it was much lighter, almost as if it had been erased fast. It was next to *compensator*. I read the definition: "*n*. 1. One who or that which compensates; esp. a mechanical device or a substance used to compensate."

Of course, I told myself, Conner was only a mechanical device. He couldn't move, he had no hands to turn dictionary pages, no eyes to read with, and no way at all to make these two light, neat pencil checks in the dictionary. I rubbed them with my fingers. The darker one smudged. They were really there.

FIVE

So THERE ARE A FEW other weird things about me you might as well know right now. (I mean, besides me having a crazy granddad, a dad who calls me names, a compensatory program, no friends, and a loyalty to a baseball team that always loses.)

So I'm younger and shorter and skinnier than anyone in my class, except Jane Nussbaum, and she's almost a midget. This doesn't make me really popular with the girls, except maybe Jane Nussbaum.

Personally, I still don't see the point of it. Don't get me wrong—I don't much like school, and cutting out two years seems a good idea. But not at the front, where things start. And not just to me, so that I'd be the shortest and the youngest boy in my whole grade. And anyway, what's the rush? My dad says now I'll be able to support him sooner, but that doesn't sound like a treat.

And another weird thing about me is even if I'm younger than the other guys, I've always liked girls. Maybe that's because I spent so much time hanging out with my mom, but girls have always seemed interesting to me. Especially girls like Donna Ames. She has this long blond hair that's all curly. She kind of leans on one leg and tosses her head back and her hair goes all over. She's really cute, and she knows it.

Now, there's no chance that Donna Ames, who is just about the most popular girl in the whole school—with girls, not just with guys— is *ever* going to go out with me. In seventh grade she had a boy-girl party at her house and I wasn't even invited. I told myself it was because The Accident just happened and everyone was treating me kinda weird then, but probably it was because Donna didn't know I existed. But I thought about her, even if she didn't think about me. And I could make her laugh. Once when her best friend, Jennifer Santucci, was out sick, she said she missed her, so I did a perfect Jennifer Santucci imitation (it was easy—she has a lisp) and said

I'd fill in for her. I sat with Donna all through lunch and talked like Jenni and asked questions about "outfits" and "athethories." Donna couldn't stop laughing. And once I figured out her locker combination and hid in it upside down until she opened the door. She screamed.

"Oh, Pollard, you're so weird," she said, and laughed. Like I told you, my mother used to say that. Donna is definitely very beautiful for an eighth grader.

The last weird thing about me is my gallery on the landing outside my room. It's on the wall behind Scarlett "Anklets" O'Hara. I started it after The Accident, with clippings from the newspaper, but I didn't mean it to become so major. I just started scanning the newspaper to cut out Mafia and Italian articles before my granddad saw them and went apejack on me. I began to notice articles that struck me as really nuts. Like one was about a policeman from Levittown who killed himself. The reporter interviewed his wife, and she said, "Jim was very happy. We had no problems. I don't know why he did this." Then there was the teenager who came home from college and shot his whole family over the Thanksgiving weekend. "He was a wonderful boy. He always got good grades and he loved his folks," his uncle Ed said in the newspaper. Then there was a man who walked into the real estate office where he worked and shot his boss and himself in front of all the other people. One of the witnesses said, "He was an excellent broker. We don't know what happened."

Every week, it seemed, there was another one of these stories. And that's not counting the really famous Long Island stories, like Amy Fisher and that guy who kept killing women. Maybe it's something about Long Island that makes you crazy. Anyway, these stories were really strange. I started to cut them out. Then I glued one to the wall in the upstairs hallway next to the clipping of Gonzo playing Frisbee. My dad never came up to the third floor, so I figured it didn't matter. Soon my gallery filled up both walls and started to overlap. It was weird and I knew it, but I kept doing it. I don't know why.

The Monday after Easter break, I was the first guy to school. Partly it was curiosity, but also it had been a really boring vacation. The Sox looked pretty boring, but the Yankees did too: Don Slaught hadn't come back from his elbow injury and they didn't have another catcher.

34

Anyway, it had been a pretty grim Easter. Just me, Granddad, and the microwave, cooking frozen dinners. If anything, Granddad seemed to be getting worse. He was calling me "Vincenzo" now, and I was afraid he was going to stop eating again. He did that once before and my dad took him to the doctor, but Grandpa just spit out the pills.

Once, over the weekend, my dad did ask me if I wanted to go grocery shopping with him, but I wasn't really in the mood. I mean where's the fun in tooling around Waldbaum's on a Saturday night, filling the cart with Pop Tarts and chicken pot pies? I know my dad probably got hurt feelings, but I couldn't face it. Let's be honest: Only a loser does his grocery shopping on Saturday night.

So other than Conner and my gallery, I hadn't had much to do or think about. Occasionally I thought about flunking, but the funny thing was that even though I was so bored, I didn't do any of my homework. I was failing language arts and I wasn't doing too good in U.S. history, and I had a report due, and even though it gave me butterflies in my stomach when I thought about it, I *still* didn't do it. And even though I could just imagine Mr. Mead's glittery eyes when he asked me for my history report and I didn't have it, I *still* didn't do it. I guess my dad is right: Sometimes he looks at me and snaps, "Where's your head? Lost on the Mediterranean?" Only the Mediterranean sounds like it would feel good, and this definitely felt bad.

Sunday night I had a really weird dream. I dreamed I was dancing with Scarlett O'Hara, but she wasn't a mannequin. She was real, and her skin felt so soft. I was holding her around and we were dancing in big, loopy, circles. I was feeling better—really weird. And then she danced away from me and I knew I would never be close against her again.

I woke up and the bed was wet. You know what I mean. It took me a long time to fall back to sleep.

On Monday morning, after the so-called holiday, I waited for Mr. Hanson, the janitor, to open the doors. I had that sick feeling in my stomach: You know, the one you get before a test when you haven't studied? I'd set my alarm early so I could wake up and do my U.S. history paper, but I'd used the snooze button for two hours. I hadn't done my homework, but I did finally get up and was here earlier than anybody else. At last Mr. Hanson showed up and opened the doors and I ran up to the computer lab. It was empty, of course. I walked over to the Mac. I slipped the disk in. Before I had a chance to do anything, the screen lit up.

YO, POLLARD. NICE TO SEE YA.

IS THAT YOU, CONNER? I typed.

YOU WIN THE PRIZE.

Great! Just my luck: I get a sarcastic computer. LISTEN, I WONDERED EXACTLY WHAT A COMPENSATORY PROGRAM *DOES*.

NOT *A* COMPENSATORY PROGRAM, POLLARD. *YOUR* COMPENSATORY PROGRAM. I DO PRETTY MUCH WHATEVER YOU NEED DONE.

That was fishy right there. I mean, I'm a kid. A short, skinny underachiever. Nobody ever cares about what I need.

HOW DO I KNOW YOUR NOT A SPY? I typed.

I THINK YOU MEAN "YOU'RE," AS YOU ARE CONTRACTING THE WORDS *YOU* AND *ARE*. OTHERWISE *YOUR* ONLY INDICATES POSSESSION, AS IN "I DON'T LIKE YOUR ATTITUDE."

Great! A grammar correction. Just what I needed. THANKS FOR THE SPELLING LESSON, CON, I typed. MEANWHILE, ARE YOU A SPY OR WHAT?

MAY I ASK IS "CON" A NICKNAME BY WHICH YOU ARE ADDRESSING ME?

YEAH. SO?

I AM DELIGHTED! I THINK SOBRIQUETS OR

NICKNAMES INDICATE FRIENDSHIP. ARE WE FRIENDS ALREADY?

NO. AND MY NICKNAME IS DULLARD AND ONLY MY ENEMIES USE IT.

OH, I AM SORRY. I WAS TOO FORWARD. I APOLOGIZE.

Somehow, believe it or not, I felt kind of bad that I was being so cold to the guy or compensator or program or whatever he was. But then I thought that might be a trick to win me over.

ARE YOU A SPY? I typed in again.

FOR WHOM WOULD I BE SPYING?

I know that old trick of answering a question with a question now, but back then I didn't.

I DON'T KNOW, BUT SOMETHING'S FISHY. MAYBE YOUR A SPY FOR MR. MEAD.

I THINK YOU MEAN "YOU'RE." AND THE ANSWER IS: CERTAINLY NOT, POLLARD. THE MAN'S A HACK.

WELL, FOR JORGENSON, THEN.

I'M AFRAID HE'S FAR TOO PEDESTRIAN TO EVER THINK OF SUCH AN INTERESTING ARRANGEMENT.

WELL, MY LIFE'S TOO PEDESTRIAN TO HAVE A SPECIAL PROGRAM IN IT.

REALLY? I HARDLY AGREE. BUT IF IT'S SO PEDESTRIAN, WHY WOULD ANYONE SPY ON YOU? He had me there. His bright line of type paused, then continued. HEY, POLLARD. I THINK YOU'VE BEEN REALLY SAD. AM I RIGHT?

DON'T YOU THINK THAT'S GETTING TOO PER-
SONAL?

I ALREADY EXPLAINED THAT I AM A VERY
PERSONAL COMPUTER, POLLARD.

I LOOKED YOU UP IN THE DICTIONARY.

THAT WAS UNNECESSARY, POLLARD. BUT SUR-
PRISINGLY ACTIVE. I THOUGHT YOU HATED USING
THE DICTIONARY. I CONGRATULATE YOU ON YOUR
INITIATIVE, THOUGH. I REMIND YOU THAT I AM
FULLY LOADED WITH A DICTIONARY FUNCTION, SO
YOU DON'T HAVE TO BOTHER. FAR MORE EFFICIENT
AND JUST AS COMPLETE.

OH YEAH? WELL IF I LOOKED UP "COMPENSATOR"
ON YOU, WOULD IT BE COMPLETE WITH A LITTLE
PENCIL CHECK NEXT TO IT? That slowed him
down for a few seconds, which is a long time
for a Mac computer.

IS THERE A CHECK BESIDE "COMPENSATOR" IN
YOUR DICTIONARY? he asked. It felt good to
have *him* asking the questions for a change.

YES, AND NEXT TO "COMPENSATORY" TOO. ISN'T
THAT AN ODD COINCIDENCE?

GOOD USE OF SARCASM, POLLARD. NICELY
POINTED. WHAT ELSE DID YOU LOOK UP? he asked.
At the time I didn't notice that he was avoid-
ing my question. But despite the compliment,
don't think I was completely dopey. I was still

on guard. In fact, it seemed kind of creepy, him asking that. Like *he* was checking up on *me*.

NONE OF YOUR BEESWAX, I typed. All right, it was pretty stupid. Next I'd be telling him to stick his head in gravy. But I was nervous. After all, this thing could have been a Russian or a hallucination I was having or even the devil that decided on a more up-to-date way to do his stuff. My granddad always says computers are the devil's work. But I believe that devil stuff is dumb. I think my granddad says that about anything that makes him nervous.

POLLARD, I EXPECT IT WILL TAKE A WHILE FOR YOU TO TRUST ME. I'M PREPARED TO WAIT. IN THE MEANTIME, WHY DON'T YOU CHECK ME OUT? ASK FOR SOMETHING YOU WANT.

I didn't stop to think, I just typed. I WANT MY U.S. HISTORY PAPER DONE.

SUBJECT? Conner asked.

THE IMPACT OF THE WAR BETWEEN THE STATES UPON THE ECONOMY OF THE SOUTHERN STATES.

HOW MANY WORDS?

SEVEN HUNDRED AND FIFTY.

The Mac was silent for a minute. The screen was dark. Not even a flicker. Then the printer began to chatter like a squirrel. I jumped. In the silence of the computer lab, it startled me,

I can tell you. Remember, all this "talking" Conner and I had done was strictly silent on the screen. I walked over to the printer.

HOW WE LOST THE WAR AND LOST OUR FARM
by Lanier Sinclair Packworthy
as told to Pollard Ian Gunning

That's what it said across the top. Then it was a story told by this sixteen-year-old Confederate boy who lived in Virginia during Civil War times. It was also about how his father and his brother died and how he and his momma and his grandpa managed to keep the farm running through the war and then how all their savings, in Confederate dollars, were declared worthless and how they had to sell their house and go and live in Richmond and be poor relations to his momma's family. It was a terrible story and you can see how badly hurt poor Lanier Sinclair Packworthy was. He was angry too, I can tell you. You could tell from the irony he used when he talked about Reconstruction. I was really interested in it. I read all the pages as they printed out and then I went back to the Mac and sat down at the keyboard.

YO, CONNER. THAT WAS GREAT. HOW DID YOU

41

KNOW ALL THAT ABOUT LANIER SINCLAIR PACK-
WORTHY?

NONE OF YOUR BEESWAX. You have to admit
that, for a computer, he was pretty funny.

THANKS, CON. I typed. IS THIS ORIGINAL? I
MEAN, I CAN HAND IT IN AND NOT GET CAUGHT?

DON'T MENTION IT, POL, he answered. IT WAS
ALL ACCURATELY RESEARCHED. SOURCES ARE
LISTED ON THE LAST PAGE. AND I FIGURE YOU'LL
GET AWAY WITH IT. I USED SOME OF *YOUR* SPELLINGS.

It was almost nine o'clock. I could hear all
the noise in the hallway. The butterflies in my
stomach had finally stilled. I took "my" homework, of course. I couldn't wait to hear what
old Mr. Mead would say about Lanier Sinclair
Packworthy. I can't say that I paid much attention in class, but that was nothing new. What
was new was that I was kind of happy thinking
about Conner. Who *was* that guy? Or *what* was
he?

The smartest guy in all Matzoh-Pizza is John
Osborne Saurey. He lives next door to us. He's
my age, but because he hasn't been skipped,
he is only in sixth grade. They wanted to skip
him, too, but his mom wouldn't let them. He
is also crazy. He has a mother who is so fat that
she can't drive a car. He goes to a psychiatrist
and he insists that everyone call him by his

full name. For some reason, they do.

John Osborne Saurey knows everything about computers. And he was like a world champ at Dungeons and Dragons and all the computer games. Plus he programmed, and he had won regional science prizes twice. Like I said, he is smart, but I didn't want to hang around with him because he is young and weird too. It would ruin me in the eighth grade.

He and his mom sometimes bring food over. And he is the only kid, aside from Jane Nussbaum, who still makes an effort and talks to me. "They'll probably send you to a shrink now," he told me after The Accident. John Osborne Saurey was usually always right. "If you want, I'll measure your head before you have to go to be sure they don't shrink it too much." He kind of smiled. "I liked your mom, Pollard," he said. "I'm sorry." He is kinda okay for a weirdo.

So I figured maybe I could ask John Osborne Saurey about this computer thing. But first I figured I'd try the library one more time. After all, I didn't need to be walking down the street with John Osborne Saurey and bump into Donna Ames.

It wasn't until Monday afternoon that I got a

chance to go back to the library. "Well, Pollard. You're becoming quite the scholar of late," said Miss Groten. She always talks like that. She is so lame. I just smiled at her and walked over to the dictionary. First I looked up Conner. Of course, I know it is a name, and proper names aren't usually listed. But it didn't really sound just like a name. It was more a word-sounding name than a name-sounding word, if you get what I mean.

Sure enough, there on page 387 was an entry. CONNER *(kon'-ner) n. (from ME cunnen; AS cunnian, to try, test, examine.)* An examiner; one who inspects or tests. *(Archaic)*

I didn't get it. Conner wasn't testing me. At least it didn't seem that way then. And "archaic" meant out of date, real old. Conner was a Mac PERMA Series, the newest of the Apple line. It was confusing.

I don't know why I did what I did next. There was no particular reason for it. I certainly didn't think anything would change. I just flipped back to page 370, where I'd looked things up last week.

The pencil checks were gone.

SIX

JOHN OSBORNE SAUREY
had been right. When I came back to school
after The Accident and my getting sick, I had
been sent down to Jorgenson, who gave me a
note to take to what I called the Mental Health
Barn. It made me mad.

"I'm not nuts!" I had said angrily. "I had
pneumonia, not a brain tumor."

"I don't think you're nuts, Pollard. And this
has nothing to do with your pneumonia. I just
think that our standard operating procedure
of sending trauma victims to the clinic makes
a lot of sense."

Trauma victims. I *really* hated that. *Victim* is
like the most disgusting word. You got to hand
it to Jorgenson: He's got a really sensitive

touch. He told me to cut gym class and head over there.

What do you call a trauma victim on his way to the Mental Health Barn? A Pollard.

The first time, I was real nervous, I gotta tell you. So I was walking and whistling the tune from that really cool movie about the prisoners of war in World War II who built a bridge for the Japanese. Then I started to sing it, but with different words: "Comet, it makes your mouth turn green! Comet, it tastes like gasoline! Comet, it makes you vomit! So eat your Comet, and vomit today!"

It was, like, a totally childish thing to be singing, but it made me feel better.

The Mental Health Barn isn't at McKinley Memorial. It's over by the Old Town Hall building. I didn't want anyone to ever see me going in there. I mean, I may be kind of un-happy, but I'm not a feeb. Plus my granddad says that those psychiatrists can see what you're thinking and read your mind. I mean, I know *he's* whacked-out, but it can still make you nervous, you know.

Anyway, the first visit was a big nothing. I just filled in a lot of forms, and then this guy came in, he didn't even say hello or tell me his name, and he gave me this stupid test where they gave you the beginning of a sentence and you had to put in the end. It was real boring.

I had another appointment scheduled. Of course I still didn't really feature the idea of anyone seeing me going into the cuckoo clinic. Today, I kind of hung around across the street in the Frank's Hobby Shop doorway until the coast looked clear. Then a wild thing happened. I thought I saw my mother cross the street and walk into the clinic. Now, that's really nuts: A, because she's dead, but also B, because she always said she'd wanted to be a shrink. (And she used to call *me* weird.)

So I tried to calm down, which wasn't easy. I walked across the street, breathing deeply. I know the way this stuff works because of what John Osborne Saurey told me and I wasn't going to play. He told me about an inkblot test they use to see if you're nuts. Like one of the blots will look like your mother or something and if you say that and start crying, then they get you to talk about your mother, and I wasn't going to do it, not with some doctor who'd call me a mental. And I wasn't going to cry; I was certain of that. Plus, if they asked about home, they might find out about my granddad, and that would mean they'd stick him in a bin for sure.

So when this kind of fat, blond woman, who was kind of pretty even though she was fat, came to the door of the waiting room and looked at me, I was surprised when she smiled real nice and said my name.

"I'm Sue Brandon," she said. "May I call you Pollard? You can call me Sue." There was no doubt that she was chunky, but still cute for an old person. She must have been way over thirty. Older than my mom, anyway. "I'm a social worker, and Mr. Jorgenson suggested we talk."

I walked into her office. Two chairs, a desk, a wastepaper basket, a crowded bookshelf. A picture on the wall of two boys lying in a field of wheat. "So, are you going to give me those ink tests?" I asked. I didn't call her anything. I wasn't sure if a social worker was a shrink or not. I'd have to ask John Osborne Saurey.

"Rorschachs?" she said, sounding surprised. I didn't know what she was talking about. "You mean blots?" I nodded. "Do you *want* to?" she asked. She sounded even more surprised. I wondered if I was doing something wrong already.

"Sure," I said. I didn't want her to think I was afraid. But I was. Because I was starting to think I *was* nuts, and if she thought so too, I knew it was all over.

"Perhaps we could talk awhile first," she said. She did have a really nice voice. "What made you think of the inkblot tests?"

Uh-oh. I could see the trick already. If I told her John Osborne Saurey told me about them, then I'd have to tell what he said and what I thought, and then I'd have to talk about my mom. Screw that. If I told her I'd just *seen* my mom, then she'd certainly lock me up in the bin. "I don't know," I said.

"How's school?"

"Okay. I mean, I'm not doing too good right now, but I'm going to catch up soon."

"And how are things at home?"

"Fine." I thought about those meals with Granddad. *Creepy* was probably a more accurate word than *fine*, but I wasn't going to talk about it. "Let's do the blots," I said. I mean, I had to say *something*.

The first blot really didn't remind me of anything. Maybe two ducks facing each other, kissing. But kissing was a bad subject and ducks were stupid. I stared at the picture. Maybe it looked a little bit like my father lying in his recliner in front of the TV. But I wasn't going to talk about him, either. "It doesn't look like anything, really. Just a blot," I said. She nodded. I told her the second card looked like a tree. She wrote something down. But the next card looked exactly like Gonzo. I mean, it had his pointed ears, the cuts just below his nose, everything! It didn't just *remind* me of him, it was almost like a silhouette portrait.

"Is something the matter, Pollard?" she asked. "Are you all right?"

I managed to get to her wastepaper basket before I threw up.

SEVEN

I SPENT THE REST OF that morning at the nurse's office. At least I missed Mead's classes. Mostly I dozed, or lay there quietly. The Comet song kept coming back into my head. For lunch I drank some ginger ale. After lunch, the nurse woke me up and said she'd call my father to pick me up.

"It isn't necessary," I said. "I feel much better. It must have been the leftover anchovy, goat cheese, and broccoli pizza I had for breakfast. Plus I got lots of homework to do." I think the idea of cold anchovy, goat cheese, and broccoli pizza got to her. I don't know where I got the idea from, but it worked. She let me go.

First thing I did was drop off my homework in Mr. Mead's room. Usually he's out the door like a bolt of lightning at three o'clock, but he was just getting his coat when I came in.

"Ah, the invalid," he said. "I figured it was the homework disease." He thinks that's sarcastic. I tried to look kind of innocent and weak, which wasn't too hard, and handed him the papers.

His face showed how surprised he was but he tried to be cool. "And typed, I see. Well, at least you made an effort." He took the paper and made a beeline for the parking lot. What do you call a lazy, sarcastic teacher with halitosis? Mr. Mead.

So, since I had nothing else to do, I went up to the computer lab. I kept thinking about Conner. I mean, where did he come from? Someone had to program him, assuming he *wasn't* a spy or from outer space or something.

The lab was quiet as usual. I found the disk in my backpack—which is completely against the rules of where to keep them—and sat down at the Apple screen. Before I did anything, before I even put in the disk, the screen lit up.

YO, POLLARD!

YO, CONNER!

HOW'VE YOU BEEN?

NOT SO GREAT. DO YOU KNOW WHAT PUKING IS?

52

A SLANG SYNONYM FOR REGURGITATION, ISN'T IT?

YOU GOT IT. I JUST DID IT AND BELIEVE ME, YOU'RE NOT MISSING A THING.

IT IS ONE OF THOSE HUMAN BIOLOGICAL FUNCTIONS THAT I WAS NOT MADE TO PERFORM, LIKE EATING. AND ELIMINATION. AND PROCREATION. SOME, I BELIEVE, ARE EXTREMELY PLEASURABLE.

It kind of made me feel creepy, Conner talking like a science fiction robot, so I changed the subject. Anyway, I had so many questions, I figured the first thing to try was to just ask them.

WHO MADE YOU?

INFORMATION UNAVAILABLE.

DOESN'T THAT MAKE YOU CONFUSED? YOU DON'T EVEN KNOW HOW YOU WERE MADE!

SO WHAT? NEITHER DO YOU.

SURE. MY PARENTS MADE ME. (It was kind of gross, thinking about that.)

YOU HAD GONE ON TO ANOTHER QUESTION— NOT *WHO* MADE YOU. *HOW*.

I KNOW ALL ABOUT THAT STUFF. WE CALL IT SEX.

I AM AWARE OF SEXUAL REPRODUCTION METHODS AS WELL AS CELL DIVISION, AND I HAVE A COMPLETE PROGRAM ON GENETICS. BUT AS I UNDERSTAND IT, NO ONE DOES QUITE KNOW *WHY* THE ZYGOTE COMES ALIVE WHEN THE SPERM AND

EGG MEET, OR WHERE THAT LIFE COMES FROM. THERE ARE THEORIES RANGING FROM GALVANIC ELECTRICITY TO GOD. WHICH DO YOU SUBSCRIBE TO?

Well, he had me there. I had to read the screen twice before I could answer, and then I could only type: I DON'T KNOW.

I REST MY CASE. YOU DON'T KNOW EITHER. ACTUALLY, FOR ME, THERE IS A DISCRETE ANSWER: SOME HUMAN DID CREATE ME. FOR YOU, HOWEVER, IT'S AN ENDLESS MYSTERY. YOU, AND ALL HUMAN BEINGS, BEGIN WITH A MIRACLE, POLLARD. IT MUST GIVE YOU GREAT PLEASURE TO CONTEMPLATE. OF THAT OPEN LOOP I AM ENVIOUS. IT ALLOWS FOR EXPANSION OF THE IMAGINATION, OF WHICH I HAVE NONE.

I thought about all that for a couple of minutes. I could believe that my mom was a miracle, but Mr. Mead? I read the screen again. That was a big advantage of computer conversation, I was realizing: You could reread it before you answered.

YOU HAVE NO IMAGINATION? I asked.

NOPE. YOU, ON THE OTHER HAND, ARE EXTREMELY GIFTED IN THAT DEPARTMENT.

BIG DEAL. SO I GET IN TROUBLE AND I DAYDREAM TOO MUCH. I'M ON THE MEDITERRANEAN. MY DAD SAYS IT WASTES MY TIME.

54

NONSENSE. A FERTILE IMAGINATION IS THE JUMPING-OFF POINT. THINK OF LIFE WITHOUT NEW IDEAS, WITHOUT DAYDREAMS, WITHOUT PAINTING, WITHOUT FICTION. THINK OF LIFE WITHOUT DREAMS.

This kind of put a new face on things. Anyway, it was nice to hear all that praise. I guess since The Accident, no one has praised me, and what with my father, Granddad, Mr. Mead, Mr. Jorgenson, and everything else, there sure have been plenty of complaints. But thinking about The Accident reminded me of my mother, and that reminded me of seeing her on the street by the clinic and how maybe I was crazy. Maybe I was even imagining this conversation with Conner. It made me sick to my stomach again but, luckily, this time there was nothing to throw up.

SOMETIMES IMAGINATION CAN MAKE YOU NUTS, I typed.

WELL, IMAGINATION MUST BE HARNESSED, Conner answered. IT MUST BE CONNECTED UP TO YOUR OTHER PARTS—YOUR DISCIPLINE AND YOUR INTELLECT. *AND* YOUR FEELINGS.

I DON'T FEEL MUCH ANYMORE, I typed. AND I'M BECOMING A TOTAL DULLARD. MY DAD WAS RIGHT.

WELL, WHO HAS BEEN PROGRAMMING YOU? WHERE ARE YOU GETTING YOUR INPUT FROM? YOU

KNOW WHAT WE COMPUTERS SAY: "GARBAGE IN, GARBAGE OUT," Conner responded. YOU ARE VERY BRIGHT. DO YOU THINK I'D BE JUST *ANYBODY'S* COMPENSATORY PROGRAM? AND IF YOU'RE NOT FEELING MUCH RIGHT NOW, PERHAPS IT'S BECAUSE YOU'RE NUMB. LOSING ONE'S MOM IS HARD ON MOST GROWN-UPS WHO HAVE HAD THEIR MOMS FOR FIFTY YEARS. IT'S EVEN HARDER ON A KID. AND IF YOU'VE HAD NO ONE TO SHARE THE PAIN WITH, IT SORT OF GETS LOCKED UP INSIDE. IT NUMBS YOU. YOU'VE GOT TO LET IT OUT, AND YOU WILL, WHEN THE TIME IS RIGHT.

I had a hard time reading that on the screen. I had to start over a couple of times, because I kept losing my place and then it seemed real blurry and hard to read.

I don't really like to write about this part, but I am. I mean, why bother to write any of this down if I'm going to be worried about you thinking I'm stupid? Or nuts? Because lots of what happened last year seems real embarrassing.

So I don't know. All of a sudden everything just started to get to me. I mean, Conner, and thinking I saw my mom, having to go to the Mental Health Barn, and the inkblot of Gonzo and the noises my granddad made when he ate and even Ms. Brandon's kind of round face and throwing up in her wastepaper basket. I didn't plan it, 'cause if I knew it was going to happen, I would have gotten out of the lab fast. But I got kind of frozen instead, and I started to cry. And not just a couple of tears out the side of my eyes, either. I mean, with noise, and a lot of snot, or phlegm or whatever you're supposed to call it—I was crying so much I wasn't even embarrassed at first—I was just kind of gone.

What brought me back was the noise. It was kind of this wooing sound, and it was real loud and high. After a little while I looked around and, since no one else was there, I realized *I* was making the noise, and I got scared. I mean, it *is* scary to be making a noise and not even know it. If it's never happened to you, you don't know. Trust me, it's really scary.

Of course, crying like that it was impossible to see what Conner was doing. I was glad he couldn't see me. I wiped my eyes and my nose on my sweater. (Okay, it was gross, but what else could I do? I mean, I was a mucus face.)

THERE IS A BOX OF KLEENEX IN THE BOTTOM DRAWER OF THIS WORK STATION.

I don't know how he could know I was crying, but he knew. He was right about the Kleenex being there too. I blew my nose, which I never do in public. When I do, it really sounds loud. I'll probably never be able to get married because of the way my nose sounds when I blow it. I hoped Conner couldn't hear as well as see. I looked at his screen. It looked real kind.

I THINK I'M GOING CRAZY, I typed.

I KNOW THAT'S WHAT YOU THINK. BUT YOU'RE NOT CRAZY.

HOW DO YOU KNOW?

I KNOW LOTS OF THINGS, REMEMBER? YOUR MOTHER'S MAIDEN NAME. PAUL'S ADDRESS IN ARKANSAS. BELIEVE ME, I BASE MY JUDGMENTS ON DATA. IT'S HOW I'M BUILT. SO BELIEVE ME WHEN I TELL YOU THAT. YOU'RE JUST RECUPERATING FROM LOTS OF STUFF. YOU'LL BE OKAY EVEN IF YOU DON'T FEEL IT RIGHT NOW.

OH YEAH? WELL, I'M SEEING THINGS.

LIKE WHAT?

I wrote about the check marks in the dictionary disappearing, and my dream with Scarlett O'Hara, and what had happened at the clinic, seeing my mother and then all that with Ms. Brandon and the Gonzo card. I didn't think it was polite to include Conner as one of the crazy things I might be imagining, so that's all I mentioned, but it was enough.

SO YOU THINK YOU'RE NUTS, HUH?

YEAH. WELL, MAYBE. BECAUSE HOW COULD I SEE

MY MOTHER WHEN SHE'S GONE? NUTS, RIGHT?

VISUAL MANIFESTATIONS BASED ON STORED INFORMATION ARE COMMON AMONG HUMANS. OFTEN, IF YOU THINK ABOUT SOMEONE, OR IF YOU TRY TOO HARD NOT TO, YOU'LL BELIEVE YOU SEE HER. IT'S A WELL-KNOWN PHENOMENON. A FAMOUS AUTHOR WROTE A STORY ABOUT IT CALLED "THE WHITE POLAR BEAR."

I DIDN'T KNOW THAT. BUT WHAT ABOUT THE BLOT? DID MS. BRANDON KNOW ABOUT GONZO? IT LOOKED *JUST* LIKE HIM.

WELL, MAYBE IT DID. SO WHAT? THAT DOESN'T MAKE YOU CRAZY.

WELL, WHAT ABOUT THOSE CHECK MARKS IN THE DICTIONARY? JUST A COINCIDENCE? IT WAS ONE CHANCE IN 149,350 OR SOMETHING. I FIGURED IT OUT.

NICE WORK. STATISTICS ARE EXTREMELY INTERESTING TO ME. ANYWAY, I'M NOT SURE ABOUT THE CHECK MARKS, BUT I HAVE MY SUSPICIONS. YOU KNOW, YOU MAY NOT BE THE *ONLY* PERSON WITH A COMPENSATORY PROGRAM.

YOU'RE KIDDING! Believe it or not, this made me feel much better, somehow. If other kids had a compensatory program, maybe I wasn't imagining all this. Maybe they were all mentals but they were looking this up in the dictionary, too. SO I'M NOT GOING CRAZY?

NO. YOU FEEL BETTER NOW?

YEAH. And it's funny, but I did. Maybe you think it's really dumb for me to take the word of a compensatory program that might be a figment of my own imagination, but I did, and I felt better.

SO WHAT ELSE CAN I DO FOR YOU?

HOW ABOUT SOME MORE HELP WITH MY HOME-WORK?

HOW DID MEAD LIKE THE PAPER?

I DON'T KNOW YET. HE HASN'T HANDED THEM BACK. BUT I'VE GOT OTHER WORK I'M BEHIND ON.

COMING RIGHT UP.

Without me even telling him, Conner began printing. In about three minutes I had my language arts sentences diagrammed, a report on Chile for geography, *and* a book report. Plus there was a science project outlined on artificial intelligence in computers. I figured Conner must know all about that.

WOW! I typed. That didn't seem really adequate, so I added, THANKS.

A PLEASURE. ANY OTHER LITTLE THING THAT I CAN DO?

HOW ABOUT GETTING ME A DATE FOR THE EIGHTH-GRADE DANCE? It was a joke, of course. But Conner didn't get it. Or maybe it *hadn't* been a joke.

60

BY A DATE, YOU DO NOT MEAN THE EXOTIC SWEET FRUIT OF THE PALM TREE. AM I RIGHT? YOU MEAN A PERSON OF THE OPPOSITE GENDER TO ACCOMPANY YOU SOMEWHERE.

RIGHT, I typed.

I sighed. When it came to reports, Conner was a whiz, but in the social scene I could see he wasn't going to have any experience.

TELL YOU WHAT I'LL DO. WE'LL HAVE A SIMULATION. THAT'S ALL YOU NEED. YOU'VE GOT EVERYTHING ELSE IT TAKES, EXCEPT EXPERIENCE. THIS WILL GIVE YOU THAT.

WHAT DO YOU MEAN? WHAT'S A SIMULATION? (Of course, now I know what computer simulations are, but I didn't then. Sue me.)

The definition appeared on the screen.

SIMULATE *(sim'-yoo-lat')* *vt.* *[<L simulare]* to give a false appearance of; feign. In computer use, to mimic or create the appearance of reality.

YOU MEAN LIKE THE VIDEO GAMES WHERE YOU'RE LIKE DRIVING A CAR? I asked.

YEP. BUT YOU'D BE LIKE ON A DATE, AS YOU WOULD SAY. YOU'D LEARN HOW. YOU DON'T THINK JET PILOTS LEARN TO DO IT BY PRACTICING IN REAL PLANES, DO YOU?

I'd never thought about it. But could Conner do a *date* simulation? And would it be embarrassing? It sounded good but scary. WOULD YOU BE THERE? I asked.

OF COURSE I'LL COME WITH YOU.

SO DO I HAVE TO CARRY YOU, OR SHOULD I PUT YOU ON WHEELS, OR WHAT? WON'T IT LOOK WEIRD TO BRING A COMPUTER ON A DATE?

I'LL JUST ASSUME A FORM. ANY FORM. WHAT WOULD YOU LIKE?

WHAT DO YOU MEAN? LIKE *ANY* FORM?

SURE. IF YOU CAN IMAGINE IT, I CAN TAKE IT ON. A CHIPMUNK. A TAPDANCING GORILLA. NAPOLEON. A PERAMBULATING REFRIGERATOR. ANYTHING.

WEIRD, I typed.

LOOK WHO'S TALKING. IF YOU CAN IMAGINE IT, I CAN SIMULATE IT. BETWEEN US, WE CAN DO ANYTHING. SO WHAT FORM DO YOU WANT?

The form that crossed my mind, to be honest, was Donna Ames, but I certainly wasn't going to mention *that*. Anyway, she'd be the girl I'd pick to have a simulated date with. And all those suggestions of Conner's seemed even weirder to take along on a date than a computer. Then suddenly I thought of Gonzo. COULD YOU LOOK LIKE MY DOG? I asked.

I thought there was a millisecond pause before Conner answered. Maybe it was just my imagination. I don't know. But I was getting more sensitive to the way he worked, and I swear he paused. Then he began blinking his message on the screen.

IF YOU EVER SAW HIM, FELT HIM, SMELLED HIM, OR HEARD HIM, I CAN USE THOSE MEMORIES TO APPEAR TO *BE* HIM IN A SIMULATION. SO WHAT DO YOU SAY?

It sounded interesting, but I'd had a long day. I'LL THINK ABOUT IT, I typed. And then, because I didn't want Conner to feel rejected, I asked WHAT DO YOU CALL A COMPUTER THAT FEELS LIKE A DOG, LOOKS LIKE A DOG, AND SMELLS LIKE A DOG?

CONNER, he wrote in big letters across the screen.

You had to like a 'pute that got your jokes.

EIGHT

I'VE NEVER WRITTEN A book before, and I don't think I'm really doing too good of a job. In real books, the story doesn't keep skipping from one thing to another and then just kind of stopping to explain stuff. Maybe real authors learn how to make it all smooth, instead of jumping around, the way these chapters do. Still, if you don't like it, you don't have to read it. I mean, it's not like you're doing a book report on it or anything. I'm just writing it so I'll be sure to remember stuff. And because of something Conner told me once about language—how it's important to write stuff down. I don't know why you're reading it. Go write your own book, if you think it's so easy. Plus I think life does skip around a lot instead of just keeping to one story. That's one thing I *don't* like about lots of books. They're not realistic.

So anyway, after all this happened in the lab, I started, for the first time in what seemed like a long time, to be interested in something. Not that much, but a little. Like I thought about Conner, and about Donna Ames, and about the idea of a simulated date. I even thought about Ms. Brandon.

At the same time, the Red Sox were starting to chalk up some games. Now, this *always* happens, but they never pay off, so I didn't want to get too excited. But I *was* interested.

Of course, don't get the idea that everything was great all at once, like the way it all works out during the last five minutes on a half-hour TV show. Mr. Mead was still a sack o' smells and I was still mostly failing and Donna Ames had not even looked up when I said hi to her yesterday outside the library.

But I did get a B plus on the U.S. history paper, and then Mr. Mead read "my" book report out loud to the class. It was wicked good, too. The book was about this kid named Huck who runs away from his mean father and lives on a raft and meets people. Conner did a great job. I felt like maybe I should really read it sometime. (Later on I did read it, and it skipped around even more than I do, but it was good and funny, too.) I had handed in the other stuff Conner did for me, and at the end of the week Miss Jalpinto gave me an A minus on my report on Chile, plus Mr. Brightman asked me to stay a minute after class and told me how interested he was in my artificial intelligence science project. But then the next Monday morning, Mr. Mead asked me to go see Jorgenson. Some reward for good behavior!

Jorgenson grinned when I walked into his office. "Well, well. Things seem to be improving."

Did I mention he has one of those lizard smiles that look like he's going to eat something? I always expect his snaky tongue is going to flick on out and whack a bug or a toad.

"I guess it wasn't such a bad idea sending you over to the Mental Health Center."

I really hate it when people gloat over something by saying "It wasn't such a bad idea." I felt like telling him it hadn't done a thing and that my compensatory program was fixing my grades, but I didn't need to spite myself *that* much.

"The third marking period ends in two weeks, and if you keep up this kind of effort, you just may pull up your grades to a C average."

Big deal, right? That would get me a scholarship to Harvard for sure.

"I was thinking you might like to pay another visit to Miss Brandon."

Puke City! It seemed unfair that when I did good, I got punished, but I knew there was nothing I could do, so I just stood there. When I'm grown up, I'm never going to pretend something a kid has to do is something he "might like." Jorgenson is such a roach bomb. So I guess he figured that if one visit had raised my grades, two might make me a genius. Keep those college acceptance letters rolling in.

"She's free at four o'clock, and I know she would like to see you then," he said.

So after school I walked over to the Mental Health Barn, and this time I didn't see anything weird until I got into the waiting room. Sitting on the fake-leather sofa was John Osborne Saurey, and he was really there, not imaginary. But weird. Truly, deeply weird.

"Wow, Pollard! This is like the Harding Avenue reunion," he said. I didn't get it. "Janie Nussbaum's in there." He motioned to another door that said "Dr. Greenblatt" on it with lots of letters and initials after his name. "Maybe it's something in the water pipes on our street that does it. Like the Love Canal."

"Does what?" I asked.

"Makes people loony," he said cheerfully.

"I'm not loony." I mean, you know I'd been thinking I *was*, but that didn't mean I liked to hear it said out loud, especially by John Osborne Saurey.

"You're here. And your grandpa's pretty loony. And my mom. And Jane's mom—she's loony *and* she drinks. But Mr. Nussbaum's okay. Maybe it's not the water, then. If it was the water, it would be universal. It could be infectious, though, like from ticks or fleas. That's how they passed on the bubonic plague, you know?"

I didn't know, and to tell you the truth, I didn't *want* to know. Gonzo used to get ticks all the time. I didn't like talking to John Osborne Saurey, because he always knew kind of gruesome stuff. He was usually right, too, but who cared? I didn't want to talk to him, now or ever. That didn't stop him.

"What you in for?" he asked.

"Huh?" I said. Pollard the Dullard.

"So who you seeing?" he explained.

"Ms. Brandon."

"Oh, Brandon. She's just a social worker. You're not in the big leagues yet. When you get seriously cracked, you'll graduate to him." He jerked his head over toward the door with the "Greenblatt" sign and the alphabet soup after it.

"What does all that stand for?" I asked John Osborne Saurey.

"M.S.W. Ph.D.?" he asked. "More Stupid Words Piled High and Deep." I laughed. He was crazy, but he was funny.

"What do you do with him?" I asked.

"I talk, he listens, and then he shrinks my head."

I knew he was joking again. I know they call psychiatrists head shrinkers, but I never really got the joke.

"In about thirty years, I'll have the same size head as everybody else and then I'll be normal," said John Osborne Saurey. Somehow, I didn't think thirty years would be enough time.

"I don't want them to shrink my head," I said.

"Oh, it doesn't hurt much. And it will do you good. You've always been too smart for your own good, Pollard."

That's what my dad always says, but John

Osborne Saurey didn't sound mean about it.

"I'm not that smart," I said. "My grades stink. I'm probably going to flunk this year." I thought of Conner then. Maybe not.

"Oh, grades have nothing to do with it. Dummies get good grades. Look at Tim Burden."

Tim was no dummy. He was captain of the baseball *and* football teams. See what I mean? Just when I was starting to let down my guard, John Osborne Saurey would say something crazy. Because John Osborne Saurey really is a crackpot. A talking crackpot.

"See, if you could be just average, or a little below, you might be happier," he explained in a voice that sounded reasonable. "At least you'd have a shot at it. But otherwise, you're doomed. You've been masquerading as one of them, but your tail's hanging out of the sheep costume."

"What are you talking about?" I asked. (Did I tell you that John Osborne Saurey could really get on your nerves?) "Anyway, I don't want them to do anything to my head. I have enough problems already."

"Okay, okay. Don't worry. Brandon probably can't shrink it much. She's only a More Stupid Words. If you want, I'll measure your head to be sure it doesn't change. I've got a really accurate set of calipers at home."

I'm sure he was kidding, but I was still glad to see Ms. Brandon's door open.

After John Osborne Saurey, it was almost relaxing to go into Ms. Brandon's office. And it was a relief to know I wasn't in the big leagues. At least not yet.

"Well, Pollard, Mr. Jorgenson says things seem to be looking up. Your marks have certainly improved the last couple of weeks." She smiled. She was trying to be nice. You could tell. "Where has this success been coming from?"

She probably wanted me to say it was because of the inkblots, or seeing her or something, but of course it was Conner. I didn't mention him to her or I *would* have been in the big leagues. I figure it's always safest to act stupid.

"I don't really know," I said. "Maybe it's because of the Red Sox."

To my surprise, Ms. Brandon nodded. "Yeah. They're looking pretty good," she said. "You think Houghton will be starting pitcher?"

I couldn't believe it. Did she follow the Sox? "Where are you from?" I asked cautiously. She

71

didn't sound like she was from Boston. She didn't say her *a*'s in the funny way my mom did.

"I'm from Sheepshead Bay, Brooklyn. I don't remember when the Dodgers left, but my dad and brothers did. After we lost the Dodgers, we never liked the Mets. Then I went off to college in Boston, and I fell for the Sox."

"Wow!" Losing a team must be rough. I mean, if there was someone you loved and they just packed up one night and they were gone, it would kill me. That's what the Dodgers did, and they had the best fans of anyone. I'm not sure I could ever root for a team after that. I'm very loyal. So I felt bad for her and the Dodgers, though I didn't respect her for switching. Anyway, we began to talk baseball. Honestly, aside from that, she didn't say anything else stupid the whole time I was there. And she didn't mention the blots or what happened last time. After a while she just walked me to the door and said, "I'm glad you stopped by. Come back anytime."

As I walked out of Ms. Brandon's office, John Osborne Saurey was on his way into the alphabet doctor's room and Janie Nussbaum was leaving it. She looked at me, but she didn't say anything and kind of looked away.

"Hello," I said. Jane was okay. I hadn't known she was loony, let alone in the big leagues, but if John Osborne Saurey said so, he was probably right. She was quiet, and really skinny and even shorter than I am, though she wasn't skipped or anything. But she's real smart. She's a kind of brownish girl—you know, brown hair and brown eyes and brownish skin that tans easily—and she's always wearing these boring clothes. She's kind of at the edge of Donna's circle, but she's not really popular. I don't think people notice her that much. I mean, she just lives across the street from me and even I never do.

"Going home?" I asked, and she nodded.

She wasn't a big talker. "Wanna walk together?" I asked. That surprised me, but I guess I was feeling good after talking to a Sox fan.

She nodded again, but this time she looked at me and smiled. She had a nice smile. Her teeth are real white. I always like white teeth.

We didn't talk at first. Twice I looked over at her. She was almost my height, which is pretty short, even for a girl. She is even skinnier than I am. What is shorter, skinnier, and loonier than a Pollard? A Janie, I thought.

It was the first time I had walked home with

anyone since Paul had moved, and the first time I'd *ever* walked with a girl, even if she was a mental case. We walked without saying anything for a while. Then Janie spoke.

"I liked your history paper," she said.

"Huh?" Pollard the Dullard. I'd forgotten all about the essay old Conner did for me. "Oh, yeah. Thanks."

"It was really good. It must have taken you a long time to write it."

I almost smiled. It hadn't even taken me a long time to *type* it, but I couldn't tell her that. "It was okay."

"I'd like to be a writer when I'm grown up," she said. Then she shut up. I think she got embarrassed or something.

"I hate to write. I'm better at math," I told her. "I'm almost flunking English."

"I can't do math. And Mr. Mokita really scares me. I *hate* when I have to do problems at the board."

"I hate when I have to read aloud."

We kind of ran out of things to hate about then, but luckily we were already on Harding Avenue.

"Well, see you around," she said.

"See ya," I answered, and she crossed the street and went into her house. It left me

74

alone in front of our place, and all at once I just didn't feel like going in. But I didn't have anywhere to go or anyone to see. Then I thought of John Osborne Saurey.

Now, I know: I said I wasn't going to hang out with him or be his friend. But I really *did* want to ask him about Conner, or virtual reality or computer simulations. Like could a computer give me a date with Donna Ames? Anyway, that was my excuse. The thing of it is, with Paul moved away and my mother not here or anything, I just didn't have anyone to hang out with. And John Osborne Saurey was right there, like a convenience store, you know. But like I didn't want to become an actual *friend* of his, because if I did, then he'd expect me to say hi in the halls at school, and maybe eat lunch with him every day, and then it would really be over for me. Tim and the guys would never be friends with me. I mean, you probably know how it is: Some kids can hang on the border of weird and then maybe climb out of it, but some also slip in, never to emerge. And John Osborne Saurey was like the King of the Land of Weird, and if I hung with him, I'd be a goner. And even when we moved up to high school, I'd still be a feeb.

See, when I was best friends with Paul, we

did stuff with other guys but *we* were the center. We weren't the most popular or the best jocks or anything, but kids hung with us because we were okay guys. And then Paul moved, and then there was The Accident and everything. And it's like the other guys must have felt bad about The Accident, but they like didn't want to just hang anymore. It was like maybe it was catching, and what I had they didn't want to catch.

It wasn't so bad, at first, being alone a lot. It felt like I was kind of in a fog, and then I'd spent most of the summer alone in my room, and that wasn't too bad.

But there's something real embarrassing about being alone in front of other people, especially when you don't want to be alone anymore. I'd been telling Tony and Brian "no thanks" for so long that they weren't offering to hang out anymore, and no one else was either. And if you've never had to walk into a crowded lunchroom and sit down alone at a table while everyone is gabbing, then you're a popular kid and I don't know why you're bothering to read this anyway.

I looked back at the house. I could see my grandpa lurking behind a curtain on one side of the living-room picture window. He opened the window. "Vincenzo," he called in his creaky old voice, "I see you there." Did I mention that I hate it when he calls me Vincenzo? It just seemed to me that if I went into that house that smelled like old beer and my grandpa's clothes, I'd lose it. It was kind of chilly outside, and there was nothing to do. I kicked a rock around to the back, until I saw my grandpa peeping out the kitchen window. If I wasn't already crazy, *he'd* make me nuts. The only side of the house that didn't have windows was the south side, which faced the Saurey house.

So that afternoon I wandered out to the side yard. All the houses on Harding Avenue and that whole part of Massapequa are split-levels and exactly alike, except for the color they're painted and the stuff in the yard. Ours had an old swing set. There was nothing in the Saurey yard. Of course, John Osborne Saurey wasn't out. He's never out. He's one of those soft, pale kids who're always inside. But since he had been waiting to see the alphabet doctor, I figured he'd be back sooner or later and I could catch him before he ducked into his house.

Sure enough, in about ten minutes he appeared.

"How are things in Glockamorra, old sport?" John Osborne Saurey is always saying weird stuff like this from a time machine or movie or something.

"You know," he said, "I was reconsidering. It can't be the water, so maybe it's the street name."

For a minute, I didn't have a clue to what he was talking about. Then I realized he was still talking about why almost our whole street was bonkers.

"What about the name?" I asked. The development streets were named for presidents: the main street was Washington Avenue, and there was Madison, Adams, Jefferson, McKinley, Polk, and Harding.

"Well, what do you know about Harding?" he asked. Without waiting for an answer, he continued. "He was a failure, the big failure president. He got caught cheating on his wife, and stealing government money, and he nearly got thrown in jail. The only good thing about him was his looks. So maybe because we live on Harding, it's like a self-fulfilling prophecy."

"What?" I asked again. Honestly, you would say it a lot too, around John Osborne Saurey.

"A self-fulfilling prophecy, old sport. It's like

if someone tells you not to trip on the stairs, and then you do."

I'd noticed that happens, especially when my father warns me to be careful.

"So you're saying because Harding was a failure, we all think we are, and then we fail?"

"Yep, that's the theory."

I thought a minute. First of all, I didn't like to admit I was a failure—I hadn't flunked yet. And anyway, he made me mad.

"It can't be," I said.

"Why not?"

"'Cause I didn't even know Harding was a failure, so how could the curse work?"

He looked at me for a minute. "Bingo, old sport," he said. "And they all say you're stupid." He smiled. His teeth were kind of greenish.

"Come on in for a spot of tea," he said, and after a quick look around to see if anyone saw us, I followed him up the cement path into his house.

NINE

HIS ROOM WAS *INTENSE*. I mean it. First of all, it was the master bedroom, the biggest in the house, and it had its own bathroom. I could see that because the door to the bathroom was removed, and you could see in there. But neither of those things was the first thing you noticed. The first thing you saw was that the walls, ceiling, floor, and even the windows were black: absolutely black, with a thick, even coating of blackness. Even his bathroom was completely black, the tiles, the sink, even the toilet. Did you even know they made black toilets? His bed was covered with a neat black spread, and the carpet was wall to wall and a real deep shag and also dead black. I could see all this as I stepped in, but it took my eyes time to adjust to the darkness, so at first I didn't see anything else.

Then I started to look around. There was a whole set of black shelves that were fixed to the wall in some way so that they just seemed to be floating. I looked at the first one, and it had about six thousand tiny figurines on it—I'd never seen so many little statues. There were owls with eyeglasses on, and a tiny mouse with wire whiskers and a cat drinking from a puddle of milk and all kinds of stuff. It was kind of corny, but there were so many of them, and they were lined up so neatly, that it was kind of impressive.

Then I leaned over to look at the next shelf and jumped when something moved. It looked like a chain from off a necklace, but then I saw one end was attached to the shelf with a sort of screw. I looked closer. The other end was moving—because it was attached to the leg of a hairy tarantula. A real one! I nearly jumped out of my skin. I mean, my nose was almost touching it!

"Ech!" I said.

"Now, now. No homo sapiens chauvinism here. Remember, to a *Barchypelma smithi* you probably don't look like Garbo."

Typical John Osborne Saurey. I didn't understand any but three or four words in *that* sentence. Still, the room was great and I wanted to look around. He showed me his comic book collection, which was enormous, and he had it all cataloged in his personal computer. And he showed me his videos—he had more than even the library.

"I'm really into films," he said, sounding kind of modest for him. "I think I'd like to be a filmmaker." But that was nothing. He also had a pretty big boa constrictor in a glass aquarium kind of thing (but no water in it, of course) and a real aquarium with black gravel and a black castle with these enormous, really freaky black fish that had their eyes in like these bubble sacs.

"They're orandas," John Osborne Saurey told me. "They're specially bred Japanese goldfish. These black ones are called moors. I guess after Othello."

I didn't know what he was talking about again, but the fish were really something— they had these long fins that waved as they moved in the aquarium light and made patterns against the walls. It was like a living light show.

I could hardly believe that this kid had so much great stuff, and such a totally unusual weird room, and that it had been next door, in a house that looked just like mine, all along. Then I thought of my gallery and Scarlett "Anklets" in the hallway outside my room, and I figured that maybe inside all the split-levels that looked just alike on the outside was real weirdness inside. I wasn't sure if the idea reassured me or made me feel worse.

Anyway, me and old John Osborne Saurey looked at more of his stuff and we talked about computers for a while, and I was just going to ask about compensatory programs when his mom called him down for dinner.

I went home, said hello to Grandpa, and popped a couple more Hungry Man dinners in the microwave. My dad almost never came home for supper, but the good thing you can say about frozen dinners is that if he *did* show up, I'd have it ready in a minute. We were down to our last three: a turkey and two chicken tetrazzini. I knew better than to give the tetrazzini to Grandpa, so I had it and the two of us ate in the kitchen. Then I went up to my room. I passed Scarlett, and in the dimness of the landing it seemed as if she smiled.

I wondered if my father would let me paint my room black if I wanted to. Of course, he probably wouldn't know if I did. He hadn't been up to my room in over a year.

I flopped onto my stomach on the unmade bed and stared out the window. Across the way I could see the Nussbaums' house. I wondered which room was Janie's, and what *her* room looked like. Probably brown and real neat, like she was. I wondered if she'd ever ask me in. It was funny—I'd lived on Harding Avenue all my life, but I'd never been in any of the other houses. Maybe people in the suburbs figured that your house was just like theirs so they didn't have to show it to you. Personally, I think it's a pretty lousy way to be. I fell asleep, there alone on my unmade bed in my clothes, and didn't wake up until it was almost time for school the next morning.

I've got to say that it was becoming a little more interesting to go into class. I didn't feel so nervous. Because I always had my work prepared now. Good old Conner was doing just about everything but my math homework (you can't type that, and anyway, I was always good in math).

It was a good thing, too, because Mr. Mead was really piling it on. He said we'd better get used to it, because this was what it was going to be like in high school. Kids just groaned. I figured I'd better groan, too, just not to be suspicious, but really I almost smiled when he'd double up chapters or assign another Shakespeare play. It was *Othello,* and he was a black guy they called the Moor. So then I knew what John Osborne Saurey was talking about with his black fish.

"You seem to be coming along with the Remedial Language Arts program, Pollard," Mr. Mead said. I had to smile. After all, if it hadn't been for Mr. Mead, I wouldn't have Conner. "How's it doing?"

"Just fine."

"I'd like to see some print-outs, please," he said. It's like he didn't trust that I was really doing it. But I was sure I could get Conner to print them. "Well, I've already seen an improvement in your homework, though I can't say your spelling in class has gotten any better." One of the problems with Conner doing my work was that it made what I did in class look even worse. So I'd started to pay attention. (That's how I knew about *Othello.*)

"I can use a dictionary at home," I said. "That helps."

"It certainly does," Mr. Mead said. "And you may see that it shows on your report card today, too. I appreciate effort. Why don't you read your composition to the class?"

So I got up and started reading my—well,

really Conner's—composition. But my mind wasn't on it. I'd completely forgotten that we were getting our report cards today. It was like I hardly ever thought ahead or planned. My stomach started fluttering. . . . What would happen now? I know I was doing better, but maybe not good enough. If I failed this marking period, I was dead meat.

Somehow, I managed to read the composition. It was supposed to be about a historical character we admired, and Conner had picked this guy Galileo. It was done like a TV interview—I was interviewing Galileo and asking him how he had figured out the world revolved around the sun instead of vice versa. And then how it felt when the Church got mad at him for saying so, and what he did. The guy was really okay, like he had been real smart and real brave, but it seemed like at the end, when he was dying, he gave in so he could be buried in sanctified ground and all.

"Was it worth it?" I asked. "If you had to do it over, would you recant?" (If you don't know what *recant* means, look it up. I had to.)

"It was my biggest mistake," Galileo said. "I deeply regret it. You see, you are dead forever—I myself have already been dead for over five hundred years—but you are only alive for such a very short time. Every second matters. Never, *never* do anything to compromise your living. That is the secret to real satisfaction."

I finished the paper and looked around the room. Donna Ames was doodling in her notebook and Tim Burden was passing a note to her. Most of the other kids were bored too. But Janie Nussbaum had craned her neck around and was staring at me; her mouth was a little bit open. When she saw me looking back at her, she turned around real fast. Her hair swung and brushed the back of her neck, which was thin and very pale. Her head bent forward, and I could see the hairs that were cut short and made a kind of V in the center, above her collar. It made me feel funny, if you know what I mean. I was glad I could sit down then.

"Bravo," said Mr. Mead. He's always saying corny stuff like that. A couple more of the kids looked at me.

After Mr. Mead's comment, I felt like I could face the report card, so in the hallway, by my locker, I pulled it out of its envelope. My stomach felt sick, but I might as well get it over with.

Five C's and three B's. I couldn't believe it!

And one of the B's was in history. A C in language arts wasn't bad at all. I mean, this was no Einstein report card, but another one like this and I'd be out of McKinley for life!

Still, I was nervous. Twice now I was called on by Mr. Mead to read "my" paper aloud. I didn't want to start being a brain—they were all weirdos. I just wanted to pass, get to be pals with Tim Burden, and go to the dance with a good date! Then next year I'd be all right.

So I went down to the lab with the report card in my pocket and a new request for the old Con-man.

YO, 'PUTE! I signed on. GREAT NEWS.

LET ME GUESS. YOU GOT FIVE C'S AND THREE B'S ON YOUR REPORT CARD.

NOBODY LOVES A SMART ALECK. My dad was always telling me that (except he didn't say *aleck*—he said something else that started with an *a*.) I paused for a minute. I didn't know exactly how to ask the next question. I wasn't sure if computers had feelings or not. HEY, CON, CAN YOU DO ME A FAVOR AND NOT BE SO CREATIVE ON MY HOMEWORK?

IS IT BEING POORLY RECEIVED? Conner flashed.

NO, NO, IT ISNT—I backspaced and deleted that and retyped—IT ISN'T THAT. BUT I'M GETTING

88

TOO MUCH ATTENTION. I JUST WANT TO BE AVERAGE.

A STRANGE AMBITION. WHY?

BEING AVERAGE IS SAFE.

IT IS MY UNDERSTANDING THAT MAMMALS CRAVE SAFETY. BUT ISN'T THERE SOMETHING YOU'D LIKE TO EXCEL IN?

I thought about that.

YEAH. BASEBALL. BUT I'M *BELOW* AVERAGE IN THAT.

WELL, YOU LIKE BASEBALL. WHY DON'T WE SIMULATE IT?

WHAT, LIKE SOME COMPUTER GAME? I didn't want to be rude, but another way I was weird was that I was probably the only kid in Massapequa who didn't like arcade games or Nintendo. I mean I didn't want to say anything to the 'pute because Nintendo could be his cousin or something, for all I knew.

THANKS, BUT I ONLY LIKE THE REAL THING—THE WOOD IN MY HAND, AND THE GRASS UNDER MY FEET AND ALL.

HEY, NO PROBLEM. REMEMBER WHAT I TOLD YOU? IF YOU EVER FELT IT OR SMELLED IT OR SAW IT, IT'S STORED IN YOUR MEMORY BANK. BATTER UP.

And then, right on the screen, a palm print appeared and it said, BASEBALL SIMULATION PROGRAM—PACKAGE B. PLEASE PUT YOUR HAND ON

THE SCREEN AND CLOSE YOUR EYES.

I lifted up my palm, and it fit perfectly against the one on the screen. And then I closed my eyes. The moment I did, I felt heat rush through my palm, move up my arm, and flood my body. "Hey, what is this?" I thought.

"Don't be afraid." It was kind of a tinny robot voice in my head—Conner's voice, I guess. "I'm just doing a volumetric diagnostic."

"What's that?"

"It's a physics check on your body—your height, proportion, muscle mass to fat. It will help me to diagnose your batting errors, if any."

If any. Ha! Little did he know.

"Look, I'm not much of a hitter. That's why I don't play."

"Well, let's see why."

And then, in the weirdest way, with my eyes still closed, I started seeing things. I was on green grass, and I could see the liming of a diamond, and home plate in front of my left foot. And in my right hand there was a bat, a real Louisville Slugger. And in front of me, on the pitcher's mound, was a guy in a Yankees uniform. He was short, squat, and ugly—and though he was the regulation twenty-two feet away, I could see that it was—I'm not making this up, now—Babe Ruth. I mean, that's not a face you can forget, right?

"You ready, Pollard?" Conner's voice asked. It was coming out of the Babe's mouth. I swear.

"Are you kidding me?" I asked. "Are you who I think you are?"

"It's a simulation of who you think it is. Who would be better at batting practice?" The Babe smiled, gave a little nod of his head and then scratched his private parts. You may not know this, but the Red Sox had the Babe on their team in 1920. They sold him to the Yankees. People say they are cursed because you should never give up the most precious thing you have. "You ready?" Conner/the Babe called.

I swallowed and nodded. "Okay, then," he said, and he wound up and pitched. I choked up tight on the bat, swung low, and missed. I felt the breeze the ball made as it whistled by me. I turned around to see it was caught by Carlton Fiske. I couldn't believe it! I had a real ex–Red Soxer, in his old uniform, catching for me.

"Okay. That was very inefficient."

"Thanks a lot."

"Let's do that again in slow motion and

you'll see what I mean."

And then the Babe wound up and let go, and the ball came sailing at me and I choked the bat, and the ball went by and I felt the breeze, *and it all happened in slow motion.* Like on television replays, but it was in real life. It was amazing!

"Now, if you held the bat higher, and not so rigidly, and if you moved your right foot forward, you could lean into the swing. Let's try it again."

So we did, in slo mo, and I tried to remember what Conner had said. But when I forgot to loosen my grip, he reminded me. Because in slo mo, there's plenty of time for coaching.

The ball came floating at me. I took a deep breath. It hung, suspended, waiting to be hit. I swung, moving my whole body with it. But there wasn't that solid crack when you know you've hit right. There was only the empty knock of a fly ball.

"Damn," I said.

"No expletives required, Pollard. Learning means mistakes. It's the nature of the process. So let's take that one from just before your swing. Move your hands a little lower and put your right one farther around the bat."

I did, and we were right back at the part where the ball hung suspended. I swung, and this time the ball connected with the center of the bat and I heard that satisfying sound of a solid hit, while the shock of it moved down the bat, into my hands, and up my arm.

"That's the boy! Now let's do it again."

And we did. We did it again and I connected, and then again, at normal speed, which was much harder, but I connected. Then I missed the next pitch. And the next. And the next.

"No problem," Conner told me. "The Babe threw you one with a spin on it. Let's practice watching the pitch."

But I couldn't watch. I was too embarrassed. I mean, I couldn't just keep missing pitches and screwing up in front of these pros, even if they were just simulations. It's like how humiliated I get in front of Tim Burden, but much worse.

"Hey, what's up?" Conner's robotic voice asked. And, of course, the more I missed, the less I could try.

"Let's just quit," I said. "I've had enough."

"Hey, Pollard. You know the difference between a pro and an amateur?" I figured I was in for a boring Mr. Mead–type lecture, but Conner just said, "The willingness to work through failure."

I thought about it.

"There's really no one watching, is there?" I asked.

"Nobody here but us circuit boards," Conner assured me.

So I tried to relax and to concentrate at the same time, and I kept trying, and after a while, I *was* hitting the pitches more often than not, and then I was hitting them most of the time. I'd feel the ball coming at me and know where it was going to connect, and when the crack came, I'd smile. After a while Conner told me it was enough for one day, but I think I could have gone on forever. Still, when he told me to, I opened my eyes and I pulled my hand back off the screen and found myself back in the lab. For a minute I was dizzy. Well, who wouldn't be?

THAT WAS RAD, I typed. It felt odd to have to communicate via the keyboard again once we had been so close. HONESTLY, THAT WAS INTENSE!

GLAD YOU ENJOYED IT. WE BURNED IN A FEW NEW CIRCUITS, DIDN'T WE?

HUH?

YOU FELT SOME NEW CONNECTIONS BETWEEN

YOUR BRAINS AND YOUR NERVOUS-SYSTEM CIR-
CUITRY. THAT'S CALLED LEARNING BY YOU HUMANS.

YOU MEAN I ACTUALLY WAS LEARNING TO BAT? I
MEAN IN REAL LIFE?

POLLARD, YOU AMAZE ME. HAVEN'T YOU BEEN LIS-
TENING AT ALL? OF COURSE SIMULATIONS CARRY
OVER INTO REAL LIFE. PRACTICE DOESN'T MAKE
PERFECT, BUT IT DOES MAKE IMPROVEMENTS.
THAT'S WHAT THEY'RE FOR. AND POLLARD, YOU DID
REALLY WELL. YOU STUCK WITH IT. GOOD FOR YOU.

I know it's really stupid, but I wished Conner
had said that while I could hear him. Tinny
and weird as his voice was coming out of the
Babe's mouth, I would have liked to hear the
praise out loud.

TEN

THAT AFTERNOON, I TOOK the long way home and stopped over at Krakatoa Motors. Now, a used car lot is nothing like a new car showroom. None of the cars have that nice, clean smell that new cars do, and most of the used cars have dings or dents or faded finishes. At least most of the cars in my dad's lot seemed to. Everything there seemed used: the faded sign, the unmatched desks and chairs in the office, even Bob Granger, the old guy that was Dad's only salesman.

As usual, my dad wasn't in—he was next door at Cuppa Java. Bob motioned, and I walked up the three cement steps to the diner door.

Dad was sitting on the stool next to the cash register. He swiveled around as I came in, but his face didn't exactly light up with pleasure. "Hi," he said. "What are you doing here?"

I didn't say anything, just sat down on the stool next to him. Gracie, the waitress, looked up from her paper. "Hello, Pollard. Long time no see." She got a rag and wiped down the counter in front of me. Now the counter smelled like the rag, which reminded me of the Comet-vomit song.

"Can I have some apple pie?" I asked my dad. He nodded.

"So, it says here that they expect a real good tourist season out on the South Fork," Gracie said. It doesn't make any difference to us: Massapequa is not exactly the Hamptons. In fact, even though Southampton is only about fifty miles away, I've never even been there.

"So what?" my father said to Gracie. "Tourists don't buy used cars."

I wanted to say that it looked like *nobody* bought his used cars, but I figured it was best to keep my mouth shut. My dad would just call me a smart aleck—or smart something else that starts with an *a*. I just took out my report card from my jacket pocket and laid it on the counter.

"More bad news," said my father, and slid the card out of its cardboard pocket. He opened it up, and his eyes flicked over it. "Well, at least there's no F's," he said, and laid the card back down.

Gracie came over and put the apple pie down beside my report card. It was a big slice. I picked up the fork and cut into the crust. It was heavy, but I managed to do it, though a glob of apple and gluey juice fell onto the counter, smearing my report card. I tried to chew the pie, but it was awful. I should have known. It tasted like the crust was two days old and the filling came out of a can. I put my fork down. My dad picked up his coffee cup and drank from it, making the same noise my grandpa makes. Maybe it's genetic.

"I need some money for groceries," I said.

"The kid thinks I'm made of money," my dad told Gracie.

"Oh, they all do," Gracie said, but she smiled at me. "Like the pie?" she asked.

"Yeah. It's great." I didn't think I could take another bite of it. "But I gotta go. Grandpa will be worried about me." Yeah, right.

My father reached into his back pocket, shifting his weight to get his wallet out. Then he gave me twenty bucks. "Make it last," he said. I nodded and folded the bill and put it in my jacket pocket.

"You gotta sign this," I reminded him, tapping the card. My mom used to sign all my report cards. I looked at the old ones from before The Accident. Dad hadn't signed one. Now he took a cheap ballpoint with a chewed-up end out of his shirt pocket and wrote his name on the line. I took the card and envelope and walked toward the door.

"See you later, Pollard," Gracie called, and I saw my dad reach for my apple pie.

The next afternoon I hung around until the computer lab was empty. I had some homework I wanted Conner to do, so I signed on. Also, since the baseball simulation I had thought about the date idea. Before I could type a word, he started.

SO WHOM SHALL THE DATE BE WITH? Conner asked. It was spooky. Like he read my mind.

For a moment, Janie Nussbaum's face kind of flashed at me, but there was no doubt that Donna was prettier. A lot prettier. But, God, it would be embarrassing if she said no, or if it all went wrong.

IT CAN BE WITH ANYONE? WILL THEY GO WITH ME?

GUARANTEED. WELL, ANYONE YOU CAN IMAGINE, BUT IT'S BETTER IF IT'S SOMEONE YOU SEE QUITE A BIT AND HAVE A LOT OF MEMORY TRACES OF.

WHAT'S A MEMORY TRACE?

THE INFORMATION STORED IN THE BRAIN—A
VISUAL, AURAL, OR EVEN AN OLFACTORY MEMORY
THAT CAN BE RECALLED SO INTENSELY THAT THE
MEMORY SEEMS REAL. LIKE REMEMBER YOU SAW
YOUR MOTHER?

I remembered, all right. WHAT'S OLFACTORY?

> OLFACTORY *(all-fak'-ter-e) adj.* of the sense of
> smell; an organ of smell.

A SMELL? I NEED TO KNOW HOW SOMEONE
SMELLS? I thought of my granddad. He has this
musty smell, kind of like wet rope. I'm not
sure if he showers. Before The Accident my
mom used to make him, but I couldn't. I don't
even try anymore.

I didn't know what Donna Ames smelled
like, but I'm sure it was good.

OLFACTORY ISN'T ABSOLUTELY NECESSARY, BUT IT
HELPS, AND I AM EQUIPPED FOR TOTAL SENSORY
SIMULATION.

I sat there thinking. Once I sat behind
Donna in assembly. Usually Tim or one of the
other guys does, but she was late, and she took
the only seat, which was an empty one in front
of me. She tossed her long, whitish-yellow hair
over the back of the chair. It took me a long
time to get up my nerve, but I leaned forward

real slow, like an inch at a time, and I touched it. It felt bristly, not smooth as it looked, but it smelled good, like some kind of flower. She never even knew I touched her.

WILL SHE KNOW? I asked now.

WILL WHO KNOW WHAT?

WILL MY DATE KNOW I WENT OUT WITH HER?

POLLARD, THIS IS A *SIMULATION*. IT WILL LOOK LIKE A DATE. IT WILL FEEL LIKE A DATE. IT WILL EVEN SMELL LIKE A DATE. IT WILL ACT EXACTLY AS THE DATE WOULD ACT. BUT IT IS *ONLY* A SIMULATION, REMEMBER? IT'S LIKE THE BASEBALL SIMULATION: YOU GET PRACTICE AND THERE'S NO RISK.

SO IF I DO SOMETHING STUPID, NO ONE WILL REMEMBER, RIGHT?

I DOUBT YOU WILL DO ANYTHING STUPID, THOUGH YOU MAY BE INEXPERT. THAT'S NORMAL. YOU HAVE NO EXPERIENCE. BUT THAT'S NOT THE SAME AS STUPID. THAT'S WHY YOU DO THE SIMULATION. I MEAN, PRETTY STUPID TO LET TRAINEE JET PILOTS MAKE THEIR FIRST MISTAKES WITH A REAL PLANE, RIGHT? ANYWAY, THE ONLY ONES WHO WILL REMEMBER ARE YOU AND I.

I'M STILL KIND OF NERVOUS.

A VERY HUMAN REACTION.

Sometimes Conner really sounded like such a complete 'pute.

SO WHAT DO I DO?

FIRST, SIT COMFORTABLY AND PUT YOUR HAND HERE.

Once again, on the screen, the outline of a hand appeared. Now I knew what that could lead to. I took a deep breath. I put my hand up, and once again it fit perfectly in the outline. It tingled.

DATE CANDIDATE?

It seemed a pretty cool way to ask the question, but I already had the answer. DONNA AMES, I typed with my free hand.

WHERE DO YOU WANT IT TO TAKE PLACE?

On the screen, a whole menu of choices appeared. School dance, movie, baseball game, bowling—lots of other stuff.

I CAN'T DANCE, I told Conner. But, of course, I wanted the dance.

ON THIS DATE YOU WILL BE ABLE TO, he said.

So I picked the school dance. Good practice, right?

IT IS TRADITIONAL ON A DATE TO HAVE A MEAL. WHERE AND WHAT DO YOU WANT TO EAT?

The choices were: Uncle Frank's, the local hangout; Pizza Hut; McDonald's; Joey's Rib House; and some other places. I picked Uncle Frank's. Did I tell you I hate pizza? It's another weird thing about me. YOU'LL COME TOO? I asked.

HOW SHALL I APPEAR? WHAT SHAPE SHOULD I ASSUME?

MY DOG'S, I typed.

There was a moment's pause. YOU'RE THE BOSS, Conner flashed.

NOW WHAT?

JUST KEEP YOUR HAND THERE ON THE SCREEN, LIKE THE LAST TIME. AND CLOSE YOUR EYES.

And then the most amazing thing happened. A house appeared on the monitor. I knew it. It was the Ames place over on Burden Lane. And as I watched, the leaves on the trees out front began to move in the breeze and a cat ran across the porch. And all at one time I began to shrink, or the screen began to grow, I don't know which, and the glass against my hand got warm and turned soft, and then it sort of melted into like a clear goop, and then I was kind of pulled through it and I was standing in front of the Ames place, with Gonzo next to me, my hand on his collar.

Amazing. "Gonzo?" For a minute, I forgot that this was just a simulation. It was Gonzo walking beside me. I knelt down and hugged him. He had that kind of doggie smell that dogs have. He turned and licked my face. His breath was stinky, like it used to really be. "Oh, Gonzo," I said. I just hugged him for a while. You wouldn't understand if you never lost a dog.

After a while I stood up. Gonzo looked at me. "You okay?" he asked in a kind of tinny, mechanical voice.

I couldn't believe it. "You're Conner," I said. For a moment I had forgotten. It kind of shook me up.

"Wasn't that what you requested?" Conner/Gonzo asked. He moved his head to the side just the way Gonzo did when he didn't understand something.

"Yeah. Yeah. It's what I requested," I told Conner/Gonzo. "So now what?"

"Go ring her bell," Conner/Gonzo said. So I did.

"Hi!"

It seemed as if Donna had been waiting at the door.

"Hi," I croaked.

"Relax, Pollard." Conner's robot voice said. I glanced over my shoulder and there was Gonzo, or Conner or whatever, standing in the yard. He kind of nodded his head to me. I was pretty sure Donna hadn't heard him.

"Nice jacket," I said as Donna stepped out onto the porch. She looked beautiful. She had on baggy jeans and a blue sweater and her jacket, which was soft and shiny.

We walked down the steps. Donna is tall. Even when she was a step lower than me, she was taller. She was about two steps ahead of me when she started to scream.

Now I've heard screaming, like when the Sox were in the playoffs, but this was like crazy stuff. It was maybe shrieking, or something like that. It was unbelievably high and shrill, like a whistle on a teakettle that had gone insane. I tripped on the step ahead of me, fell forward, hit Donna's back and the two of us were down on the sidewalk. Through all of this she never stopped screaming.

I jumped up; I mean, was one minute of a date with me enough to drive a normal girl completely crazy? Then I saw she was pointing at Gonzo.

"Is it the dog?" I asked. She kept shrieking, but at least she nodded. "Are you afraid of dogs?" I asked. She kept shrieking, lying on the walk. "Go away, Gonzo," I yelled; and he turned around and trotted down to the corner. Donna lifted her head up.

"He's gone?" she asked. I told her he was and she stood up. I was still on the ground. She was really tall when she stood up. "God, I *hate* dogs," she said.

I didn't really think there was anything in the world that Donna Ames could say that would make me not like her. I mean, she was that beautiful. But here it was, one minute and a half into our date and she had found the thing. I could feel my mind kind of twisting around. I was trying to still like her. She probably got scared by a dog when she was a baby, or something like that, I thought. And after all, it's a free country and some people just don't like dogs. And maybe she was just having a hard day or something. But even though I was making those excuses, I was shocked.

She was brushing herself off using angry little flaps of her hand. There was a twig caught in her perfect hair, but I was afraid to touch it. "So, are we like going or like just standing around?" she asked.

She sounded mad. Lots of times people who get scared act mad. My dad does it all the time. My mom explained about that. Now Donna tossed her head and her hair moved all over. It looked very pretty, even with the twig. For the first time I wondered if that was why she tossed her head so much—so people would notice her hair.

"Let's go," I said, and we started walking

toward McKinley Memorial. I didn't know what to say exactly. What do I do now? I thought.

MAKE CONVERSATION. Conner's or Gonzo's or someone's robotic-sounding voice seemed to be in my head.

"About what?" I asked.

"Did you say something?" Donna asked.

"No," I said.

"I thought you did."

"Uh-uh."

"Well, I thought I heard you. It sounded like you said 'a pot wot.'"

"What?"

"It sounded like you said 'a pot wot.'"

"What's an 'a pot wot'?" I asked.

"How should I know? *You* said it."

"No I didn't." GONZO! CONNER! WHAT SHOULD I SAY? I was careful to think it, not say it.

ASK HER A QUESTION ABOUT HERSELF.

LIKE WHAT?

MAYBE SOMETHING ABOUT HER JACKET.

"Where did you get your jacket?" I asked.

"Huh?"

"Where did you get your jacket? It's really nice."

"At the Florence Shop."

That was the expensive store in town. We got our stuff at Caldor's.

"I loved it. My mom said it was way too much money, but I was like really nagging her and I tried on every cheap jacket and said I hated them all. Usually, if I do that, she gets so tired that I can get what I want. You know?"

"How many jackets were there?" I asked. I really was curious.

"Huh?"

"How many jackets did you have to try on?"

"Oh, about a million. But that's how it is with her. She can really hold out, but I can always last longer." She looked me up and down. "You interested in clothes?" she asked, sounding surprised.

"Not really."

"I didn't think so. I just love them. Yesterday, I got the cutest outfit. The shirt has cuffs that roll up and inside they are the same fabric as the skirt."

She went on talking for a while about her outfit. I think it's kind of weird about clothes and most girls. I mean, clothes are clothes. I don't have any "outfits." But Donna always looked nice. Maybe it was because of her "outfits," but I don't think so. I think she'd look pretty in anything.

"Who's going to the dance?" I asked, just to change the subject.

"Oh, everyone. Cindy and Jennifer and Tim and Tony and Brian."

"Janie Nussbaum?" I asked. She looked at me.

"Who'd ask her?" she said.

"Not me," I said, and even though it was true, I felt mean as we both laughed.

As we got to Main Street, across from McKinley, I noticed Gonzo was still nearby, lurking behind trees and parked cars. But it's hard to hide a Great Dane behind anything smaller than a house.

"Is that damn dog following us?" Donna asked.

"I don't think so," I said. GONZO, GET LOST. BUT DON'T GO TOO FAR. AND BE CAREFUL CROSSING THE STREET. WATCH OUT FOR CARS.

IT'S OKAY, POLLARD, Conner said. THIS IS A SIMULATION. I WON'T GET HIT BY A CAR. NOW, GET READY TO BUY DONNA'S TICKET AT THE DANCE. HAVE YOUR MONEY READY.

I put my hand in my pocket and was relieved to find some dollars folded in there. Simulators apparently think of everything.

"Two, please," I said, and started to hand Donna her ticket.

NO. YOU HOLD IT AND GIVE IT TO THE TICKET TAKER. Conner's voice was in my head.

OH, THANKS, I said in my head.

Mr. Mead was standing at the door collecting tickets. Wouldn't you know it would be him! "Donna. Pollard," he said. He raised his eyebrows at me. I knew what it meant. A Pollard is *not* supposed to be with a Donna. I handed Mead the two tickets and we walked into the crowded room outside the gym.

"I have to fix my makeup," Donna said. She looked fine to me, but I nodded. I guess that's what girls do.

OFFER TO HANG UP HER JACKET.

"Should I take your jacket for you?" I asked.

"Yeah," she said. "But be real careful of it. It was *really* expensive." Like I didn't already know.

She peeled off the jacket, and I walked around the hall outside the gym until I found a hook and made sure to hang the jacket from its chain so it wouldn't tear. Then I went back to wait outside the girls' room. I waited. And I waited. I waited a long time.

WHERE IS SHE? I asked Conner. SHOULD I YELL IN THERE?

I THINK MAYBE YOU SHOULD LOOK ON THE DANCE FLOOR, Conner suggested.

I walked to the door of the gym. I could hardly believe it! Sure enough, Donna was already in there, dancing to a Michael Jackson song. I *hate* Michael Jackson's music. Donna's hair was flying all over. I think she was dancing with Tim, or maybe Tony, another guy from their gang. In fact all of them were out there on the dance floor together.

GREAT! NOW WHAT DO I DO? I asked.

GO OUT THERE AND DANCE.

I DON'T KNOW HOW.

SURE YOU DO. IT'S EASY. THIS STUFF IS JUST MOVING TO THE BEAT. THERE ARE NO RULES.

Tony was moonwalking with Donna. It didn't look easy to me.

FORGET IT. I'M NOT DOING IT. Just then the music stopped.

OKAY. SO NOW GO UP AND JOIN DONNA.

WHAT FOR? She was laughing with Tim now.

SHE'S *YOUR* DATE. ASK HER IF SHE'D LIKE A SODA OR SOMETHING.

I walked across the dance floor. I really didn't want to. Now Donna was talking to Tony and laughing. So was Tim. When I came up and stood next to them, neither of them said hello to me.

"Hey, Donna. You want a soda?"

She turned around and acted surprised to see me. Like I had dropped in from Pluto instead of from the hallway where I had hung up her coat and waited for her. "Oh! Sure.

Sure. Get me a Coke, okay?" She turned back to Tony. He whispered something to her and they both laughed. "Oh, and get one for Tony, too," she said. I nodded. And I blushed. I mean, that couldn't be right, for me to get *him* a soda. As I started to walk away, I heard Tony say, "What a feeb."

There was a long line for the drinks. I got on the end. YO, CONNER, I'M NOT HAVING A VERY GOOD TIME.

WHOSE FAULT IS THAT?

That made me think. DONNA'S FAULT. SHE DOESN'T PAY MUCH ATTENTION TO ME.

PRETTY THOUGHTLESS BEHAVIOR, IF YOU ASK ME.

I GUESS SHE DOESN'T LIKE ME.

DO YOU LIKE HER?

The funny thing is, all this time I hadn't thought about that. I mean, her skin was so smooth and her hair was so nice, and she was so pretty. I'd only worried if she liked me. And I could tell she didn't. But I hadn't thought if I liked her.

I GUESS NOT, I answered, surprised.

SO WHAT ARE YOU GOING TO DO ABOUT IT? Conner asked.

I THOUGHT YOU WERE SUPPOSED TO TELL ME.

WELL, I CAN GIVE YOU SOME PROMPTS. YOU CAN:

112

- PRETEND YOU ARE HAVING A GOOD TIME AND STICK WITH HER
- IGNORE DONNA BACK AND TALK TO OTHER GIRLS
- TELL HER YOU DON'T LIKE WHAT SHE'S DOING AND HAVE A FIGHT
- GO HOME

I knew the loser approach would just be to go home. But that's what I felt like doing. I'D LIKE TO TELL HER OFF, BUT I'M AFRAID. WHAT IF SHE LAUGHS AT ME? WHAT IF SHE GETS MAD?

WHAT IF SHE DOES?

Suddenly I felt very tired. I just lost all my energy at once, like one of those dumb clown balloons that stand up and get hit until they leak and wilt. I wilted.

COULD WE END THIS SIMULATION NOW?

OF COURSE, said Conner. YOU MUST BE TIRED.

And across the dance floor, Gonzo appeared and glided over to me. GRAB MY COLLAR, he said in that tinny voice. As everyone watched, I did, and the gym, Donna, Tim, Tony, Mr. Mead, and everyone disappeared. I had had my first date, even if it was only a simulated one.

At least I didn't have to kiss her.

ELEVEN

I DON'T KNOW ABOUT you, but I used to think tongue kissing was disgusting. I mean, I hadn't done it, so I couldn't be certain. (That reminds me of how my mom always used to say about new food, "How do you know if you don't *try*?") But I really think sometimes I just know.

So even though the guys all talked about it and wanted to, I didn't, and I guess I was kind of relieved that I didn't have to do it with Donna. It wasn't just that spit and everything is gross, but also that I don't know where the girl's tongue goes. Under mine or over it? And what if I do it wrong?

Another thing that worries me is these braces I've got. My teeth in the front were really sticking out, so Mom took me to Dr.

Krazney, who is the oldest and the meanest (but also the cheapest) orthodontist in town. He doesn't use those newer plastic kind of invisible braces, but the old metal kind that look ugly, dig in, and really hurt. I think, though, that he *liked* to hurt. I mean, even when he was just doing an exam, he'd hold this kind of horrible pick thing and poke it into my gums. I don't think it was by mistake.

So since The Accident I haven't been like wild to go back to him and my dad never notices anything—so I haven't gone. But I'm stuck with the braces on my teeth.

Bit by bit, I've been getting them off myself. I find Mary Janes work best. Tootsie Rolls don't have the pull. Starbursts are good, but I hate how they taste. Saltwater taffy is good, but it's hard to get. So it's mainly Mary Janes, which get real super-sticky and thick and I chew real slow in the back and then they pull off a bit of the brace. The bands came off real easy, and last week I got a whole circle off of my left back tooth, and the right top is a little looser, I think.

Luckily, my front teeth are already straightened out. Otherwise I'd never be able to kiss anyone without making a hole in her lip. But with these bits of metal sticking out on my teeth, I'm afraid I'd cut someone. I mean, I know I'm supposed to stick my tongue out, but does the girl do it too? I mean, what if Donna did and slashed her tongue? Like the whole idea is so gross, it makes me never want to have a date. Plus, the simulation wasn't exactly what I'd call a raving success. I felt bad.

But when I got to school and dared to look over at Donna Ames, she didn't even notice me. I guess, in spite of Conner's assurances, I was afraid she'd know about our date, but she didn't seem to. It was funny, though. I felt sad that Donna didn't like me and really rotten about looking like a dip in front of Tim and Tony, but I didn't feel ashamed or anything; maybe 'cause no one knew it happened. If it really had, or if anyone knew about it, I would die. It kind of made me not like Donna as much. And anyway, I decided until I got the rest of my braces off I wouldn't be prepared for even a simulated date.

But I still felt if the Red Sox would just once win the pennant, I could just get promoted out of eighth grade with the rest of my class, and take a girl to the dance, I would be okay, like everybody else, except for pulling off my own braces.

But I wasn't eating a Mary Jane that Thursday

in the computer lab. I was eating an apple—no, the green Granny Smith kind, not a McIntosh—and sitting at the keyboard. I had a whole bunch of homework assignments and I sat there chewing the apple. (Of course, no food is allowed in the computer lab. It's a good rule, because I hate to think of what a can of soda could do to Conner, but I was hungry and I was being careful.)

YO. YOU OLD 'PUTE, YOU.

HI, POLLARD. IS IT SAFE TO ASSUME THAT *PUTE* IS A CONTRACTION OF *COMPUTER?*

AFFIRMATIVE.

MAY I ALSO ASSUME IT IS AN AFFECTIONATE TERM?

AFFIRMATIVE.

THANKS, POLLARD. I'M GLAD TO SEE YOU, TOO. RECOVERED FROM OUR DATE?

KIND OF. IT WAS SUPREMELY LAME. BUT AT LEAST IT DIDN'T HAPPEN, RIGHT?

ONLY TO YOU, PO. ONLY TO YOU.

I liked it that he called me Po. It was like if I did something, Conner always noticed and responded. So if I called him 'Pute, he called me Po. Probably you don't know what I mean, but I liked it. Plus he remembered what I said. Maybe that was because he was a computer, but my mother always used to remember stuff I told her, too.

HOW DID THE RED SOX DO LAST NIGHT? he asked. You see what I mean?

THEY WON AGAINST CLEVELAND. BUT MAYBE YOU COULD RUN A DIAGNOSTIC ON SOME OF THEIR BATTING.

LOOKING GOOD FOR A PENNANT, PO.

DON'T EVEN MENTION IT. EVERY YEAR THEY GET ME EXCITED. THEN THEY BLOW IT.

POOR PROGRAMMING.

That made me mad. It was okay for *me* to say bad things about the Sox but not for anyone else. Not even Conner. It's like my family. I know my granddad is nuts and all, but I don't like it when John Osborne Saurey says so. It's like I put in the time with 'em, so I can say it, but other people (or even 'putes) don't have the right. Maybe I'm oversensitive or something.

POLLARD, DID I SAY SOMETHING THAT OFFENDED YOU? You gotta admit, he was really a highly alert 'pute.

KIND OF. I REALLY LIKE THE SOX.

I KNOW. I'M SORRY. I WAS TACTLESS. NOBODY LIKES TO HAVE THEIR PROGRAMMING CRITICIZED, OR THE PROGRAMMING OF THOSE THEY LOVE.

WHAT DO YOU MEAN? THE SOX, PEOPLE, THEY'RE NOT PROGRAMMED.

CERTAINLY THEY ARE. THINK ABOUT IT. HUMANS

118

AREN'T BORN WITH ALL THEIR THOUGHTS AND FEELINGS COMPLETE. THEY DEVELOP, BIT BY BIT, WITH PROGRAMMING.

WHAT? THAT'S RIDICULOUS. ARE YOU SAYING THE SOX HAVE BEEN PROGRAMMED TO *LOSE*?

SURE. SO WERE YOU. OTHERWISE WHY ARE YOU FAILING SCHOOL? YOU'RE NOT DUMB. YOU KNOW THAT. IT'S LIKE THE RED SOX. THEY'RE ALL GOOD PLAYERS BUT THEY'RE NOT PROGRAMMED TO WIN. THEY *WANT* TO LOSE.

DON'T BE RIDICULOUS. THEY DO NOT. I thought about it for a moment. IT'S NOT BECAUSE OF THEIR PROGRAMMING, I told Conner. IT'S BECAUSE OF THE CURSE. YOU KNOW, THE RED SOX SOLD BABE RUTH TO THE YANKEES AND THAT'S WHY THEY'LL NEVER WIN.

WELL, I AM NOT PROGRAMMED TO BELIEVE IN CURSES. BUT IT IS A POWERFUL NEGATIVE STIMULUS TO SELL THE MOST VALUABLE THING YOU HAVE. THE TRAGEDY OF THAT WAS THAT RUTH COST THE YANKEES SO MUCH THAT THEY COULDN'T AFFORD TO PLAY HIM AS A PITCHER. HIS TALENT WAS WASTED. *THAT* IS A TRAGEDY. THAT'S BAD PROGRAMMING FOR ANYBODY.

I'M NOT A COMPUTER. AND I'M NOT PROGRAMMED.

OF COURSE YOU ARE. IN A SENSE. YOU ARE A HUMAN BEING, NEEDLESS TO SAY, BUT HUMANS

CREATED COMPUTERS IN THEIR OWN LIKENESS. AND PEOPLE, POLLARD, *ARE* PROGRAMMED. GENETICALLY AND BEHAVIORALLY. YOUR GENES ARE PROGRAMMED TO DIVIDE AND REDIVIDE IN A CERTAIN WAY: THAT'S WHAT MAKES YOU TALL OR SHORT, DARK OR BLOND. GENETIC PROGRAMMING. AND THEN THERE IS THE BEHAVIORAL STUFF. YOU STORE UP EACH FACT, EACH EXPERIENCE. THAT'S HOW YOU LEARN. YOU AREN'T *JUST* POLLARD. YOU ARE THE SUM TOTAL OF ALL THINGS THAT POLLARD HEARD, SAW, FELT, SMELLED, OR THOUGHT.

SO IS IT "GARBAGE IN, GARBAGE OUT," JUST LIKE FOR YOU? See, I *had* been reading up on stuff in the computer lab library.

I'M AFRAID SO, POLLARD. YOUR FRIEND DONNA, FOR INSTANCE.

NO FRIEND OF MINE, I interrupted.

WELL, YOUR CLASSMATE, THEN. TAKE HER CASE: ATTRACTIVE GENETIC MATERIAL, BUT SHE HAS BEEN BEHAVIORALLY PROGRAMMED TO THINK THAT DOGS ARE FRIGHTENING, EVEN IF THEY'RE GENTLE. PERHAPS SHE WAS BITTEN; PERHAPS HER MOTHER OR SIBLINGS WERE AFRAID AND SHE LEARNED IT. IT CERTAINLY ISN'T BASED ON REAL-TIME EVENTS. THE DOG WASN'T THREATENING HER ON YOUR DATE. IT'S HER PAST PROGRAMMING.

TAKE ANOTHER EXAMPLE. SHE HAS PARENTS WHO BELIEVE APPEARANCES ARE IMPORTANT, SO THEY'VE

120

PROGRAMMED THAT BELIEF INTO HER. SHE HAS A MISTAKEN NOTION SHE IS SUPERIOR TO MOST PEOPLE BECAUSE OF HER APPEARANCE. SHE BELIEVES THIS BECAUSE FROM THE TIME SHE WAS A BABY SHE WAS TOLD SO AND SHOWN IT. BECAUSE SHE WAS PRETTY, SHE LOOKS GOOD, THEREFORE SHE MUST *BE* GOOD. AND OTHERS BELIEVE IT, DESPITE THE OBVIOUS CONTRADICTIONS OF REALITY. EVEN THOSE WHO SHOULD KNOW BETTER OFTEN DON'T. (ANOTHER EXAMPLE OF BAD PROGRAMMING, BY THE WAY.) DONNA TAKES IT FOR GRANTED THAT YOU'LL BE CONSIDERATE EVEN IF *SHE* ISN'T. DONNA JUST HAS BAD BEHAVIORAL PROGRAMMING.

ARE YOU KIDDING? I typed. DONNA IS THE MOST POPULAR GIRL AT MCKINLEY. SHE'S NUMBER ONE. THE GIRLS ALL THINK SHE'S ADORABLE AND THE GUYS WANT TO ASK HER OUT. I tried to think of other proofs. SHE'S SECRETARY OF THE STUDENT COUNCIL. SHE'S THE BEST GIRL IN THE WHOLE SCHOOL.

POOR PROGRAMMING was all Conner wrote.

I thought about the way she tossed her head, about the way she'd screamed about Gonzo even after he'd left. I thought about the mean thing she'd said about Jane, the way she'd ignored me, and how she'd told me to get a Coke for Tony. She'd even laughed when he called me a feeb. Maybe, just maybe,

121

Conner had a point. But of course, he couldn't see just how pretty her "genetic programming" made her.

WHAT MAKES YOU SO SMART? I asked.

GOOD PROGRAMMING. I swear he smirked. And he printed out a long string of stuff on the laser printer. It was weird, and I couldn't really understand most of it, but I folded the paper up and put it in my pocket. I figured it was some of his programming.

WELL, I GUESS YOU'RE NOT SO BAD, I typed.

YOU'RE NOT SO BAD YOURSELF.

There was something about Conner that made me relax. But then I remembered why I was there, and pulled out my assignment pad.

I GOT SOME MORE HOMEWORK.

I HAVE SOME MORE HOMEWORK.

YOU DO TOO? I asked. Sometimes I crack myself up.

VERY AMUSING. AS I BELIEVE YOU KNOW, I WAS CORRECTING YOUR GRAMMAR.

YEAH. OKAY. SO CAN YOU DO THESE? BUT NOTHING TOO FANCY, I warned him. I didn't want to be reading aloud again. I typed in my assignments, and Conner printed them right out.

YOU'RE AMAZING!

AN APPLE A DAY KEEPS THE FAILURES AWAY, POLLARD. I'VE GOT PLENTY OF MEMORY CAPACITY,

LOTS OF DATA TO DRAW ON, AND PLENTY OF COUN-
SELING SOFTWARE. STICK WITH ME. I'VE GOT SU-
PERIOR PROGRAMMING.

SO HOW'S *MY* PROGRAMMING? I asked.

WANT TO SEE?

WHAT DO YOU MEAN?

WE CAN TAKE A LOOK.

DON'T BE RIDICULOUS. YOU MEAN A PRINTOUT
LIKE THE ONE YOU SHOWED ME?

NO, OF COURSE NOT. WE CAN GO INTO YOUR
MIND. WE CAN SEE YOUR CIRCUITS, YOUR STORED
DATA, YOUR ASSOCIATIONS. IT COULD BE A LITTLE
BIT SCARY, BUT YOU'LL LEARN STUFF. AND I'LL
COME WITH YOU. WANT TO TRY IT?

ARE YOU KIDDING ME?

NOT AT ALL.

HOW DO WE DO IT?

NONE OF YOUR BEESWAX.

The guy was a card. I think he remembered
everything I ever told him.

THERE'S ONE THING, THOUGH.

YEAH? WHAT?

YOU NEED SOMEONE ELSE TO BE HERE.

WHAT DO YOU MEAN?

REMEMBER HOW TIRED YOU WERE AFTER THE
LAST SIMULATION? WELL, THIS IS MORE DRAINING.
SOMEONE HAS TO WAIT HERE TO TAKE YOU HOME.

YOU MEAN I HAVE TO TELL SOMEONE ABOUT

YOU? I typed. NO WAY! THEY ALREADY THINK I'M CRAZY. He could forget about that. The idea really turned me off. I mean, it wasn't really so much now that I was afraid people would think I was nuts. It was more that I didn't want to share Conner, or to have him stop just being for me. I guess I had kind of come to count on him, and not only for homework, either. Anyway, who could I ask? Grandpa? Not my dad. For a moment I thought of Ms. Brandon. But that was out of the question. We just talked baseball, and that was *all* I was going to talk to her about. Suddenly I felt something. It was a really bad and a really strong feeling. I remembered why I preferred to feel numb. 'Cause what I felt was loneliness. Big time. NO ONE ELSE COMES ALONG, I typed.

LOOK, IT'S REALLY DRAINING TO DO A SELF-DIAGNOSTIC. WHEN I DO ONE ON MY OWN PRO-GRAMMING, I CAN'T DO ANYTHING ELSE FOR A WHILE. IT USES UP MOST OF MY CAPACITY. SO YOU HAVE TO HAVE SOMEONE HERE TO TAKE YOU HOME IF YOU'RE REALLY FATIGUED.

WELL, THEN, YOU CAN FORGET ABOUT IT.

YOU'RE THE BOSS, he wrote.

I felt he was, like, disappointed in me or something, even though he didn't say it. PLUS I DON'T FEATURE THE IDEA OF WALKING AROUND IN

MY BRAIN. IT'S KIND OF A MESS IN THERE.

SUIT YOURSELF.

PLUS I HAVE NO ONE TO ASK.

OKAY.

EXCEPT MAYBE JOHN OSBORNE SAUREY.

A FRIEND?

WELL, MAYBE. HOW WOULD I KNOW?

WELL, TRADITIONALLY, FRIENDSHIP IS DEFINED AS

n. (frend'-ship) 1. The state of being friends.

BUT, MORE IMPORTANT, DO YOU LIKE HIM? DOES HE SHARE YOUR INTERESTS, THINK WELL OF YOU, CALL YOU A NICKNAME, OR SHOW OTHER SIGNS OF AFFECTION?

JOHN OSBORNE SAUREY CALLS ME SPORT. IS THAT A NICKNAME?

COULD BE. IT CAN ALSO BE USED IN THE NATURAL SENSE:

n. lusus naturae, sport of nature. A plant, animal, etc. that exhibits abnormal variation or a departure from the parent stock or type . . . a spontaneous mutation; a new variety produced in this way.

GREAT, SO HE'S CALLING ME A *MUTANT?* I KNEW THIS WOULD HAPPEN. IF YOU START HANGING OUT

125

WITH FEEBS, YOU BECOME ONE.

DEFINITION OF *FEEB*, PLEASE.

I had to think about that for a minute. FEEB *n.* SOMEONE WHO IS OUT OF IT. AN UNPOPULAR KID. A RETARD. I THINK IT COMES FROM FEEBLE-MINDED. Since knowing Conner and the whole dictionary routine, I've become more aware of word derivations.

SO YOU DERIDE PEOPLE BY COMPARING THEM WITH OTHER ONES WHO ARE AFFLICTED WITH BIRTH DEFECTS?

It sounded pretty ugly when Conner put it like that. I never meant it like that, though. IT'S JUST A WORD, CONNER, I typed. WORDS DON'T MEAN ANYTHING.

IF WORDS DON'T MEAN ANYTHING, WHAT ARE THEY FOR? He paused. HUMAN BEINGS ARE DIFFER-ENT FROM THE OTHER LIVING CREATURES ON THIS PLANET BECAUSE OF WORDS. THEY CREATE LAN-GUAGE. IT IS, IN A SENSE, WHAT MAKES YOU HUMAN. ONE OF YOUR GREAT SPIRITUAL WORKS STARTS OUT, "IN THE BEGINNING WAS THE WORD." He paused again. I THINK YOU MUST BE MISTAKEN, POLLARD.

I remembered that Tony had used *feeb* on me, and that Donna had laughed. I remembered how I felt and was ashamed.

OKAY. SO I WON'T USE *FEEB*. OKAY?

126

IT'S UP TO YOU, POLLARD.

I thought of Patrick, this kid who lived at the other end of Harding Avenue. He had Down syndrome. His brother, Kirk, was a lot older than us, and a champion swimmer. Patrick couldn't help it if he was born like that. Like Conner said, it was his genetic programming. It was pretty disgusting to make fun of someone that can't help it. And anyway, John Osborne Saurey was no feeb—he was smart. Well, I didn't mean to put it like that. Sometimes I don't know what I'm saying.

I'M CONFUSED.

THAT'S NATURAL. PUBERTY IS A CONFUSING AND DIFFICULT TIME FOR HUMANS.

God, I hate that word, *puberty*. Conner using it on me made me feel like a bug under a microscope, and lonely again.

THANKS FOR THE CLUE, SHERLOCK.

I BELIEVE THAT'S AN EXAMPLE OF SARCASM. AND A REFERENCE TO SHERLOCK HOLMES, THE DETECTIVE CHARACTER. AM I CORRECT?

AFFIRMATIVE.

SARCASM IS USUALLY A SIGN OF HOSTILITY. HAVE I OFFENDED YOU? I ONLY WANTED TO OFFER AN OPPORTUNITY FOR SELF-KNOWLEDGE.

LOOK, I KNOW WHO I AM AND WHY I AM LIKE I AM

127

AND WHY I DO WHAT I DO. WHO DO YOU THINK YOU ARE, ANYWAY? MS. BRANDON OR SOME KIND OF STUPID HEADSHRINKER?

SORRY, POLLARD. I DIDN'T MEAN TO BE PUSHY.

YOU KNOW, THAT DATE SIMULATION SUCKED. *YOU* THINK IT WAS SO GREAT? I MEAN, I DIDN'T LIKE IT.

THERE ARE MANY UNPLEASANT ENLIGHTENMENTS. I AM SORRY IF YOU FELT THE SIMULATION WAS NOT HELPFUL.

Somehow, I kept feeling worse and worse, madder and madder. So I just got up. I didn't even sign off. I just walked away from the Apple, out of the lab, down the corridor. Enough of Remedial Conner. Let him sit there. The nerve of a computer to try and tell me who I was. Like I didn't know.

As I walked by the library doors, I got a flash. It was almost time for closing, but Miss Groten was liking me so much lately that she let me in. I ran over to the dictionary, and there, on page 1393, was: POLLARD *(pol'-erd)* n. *[see poll v., poll head]* 1.a. A stag that has cast its antlers. b. A hornless animal. 2. A tree that has been cut back to the trunk to promote the growth of a dense head of foliage.

I don't know why it hit me so hard, but it just seemed funny that my name, my own weird name, was right there defined for everyone to see. And it said right there that I had no horns, that I'd been cut back. I felt like it was true, too. Tim and Tony and other guys were stags with horns, but it was like I was crippled. I was the shortest, I was the littlest. I was a stunted tree.

I stood over the dictionary for what seemed like a long time, until Miss Groten came up behind me and put her hand gently on my shoulder.

"Closing time, Pollard," she said. Miss Groten, actually, was really pretty nice. She patted my back. It made me realize that no one had touched me for a real long time. She walked back to get her coat, and I looked down once more before I closed the dictionary. And then I bent forward to look closer.

There, next to *pollard*, very, very light, almost completely erased but still denting the page, was a careful little check mark.

TWELVE

OKAY, SO I WAS FEELING lonely, and maybe sorry for myself. But there was no doubt that my life was a little bit better. Because of Conner, my grades were steadily improving, and after I got over my tantrum when I just left him flat, he and I were "practicing" baseball almost every afternoon. And I was really getting interested in the artificial intelligence science project. I mean, when you think about it, it's wild: Can we make a machine actually come alive? Think for itself? What *is* being alive, after all?

I read about it and thought about it a lot. What did being alive mean for me? And what was it for people who were dead? And what was it for Conner? I mean, was Conner alive? Could he think or was he just programmed to do whatever he was told? I tried to go over his printout of his programming, but I couldn't make sense of it. At the library there were three books listed: *The Knowledge Machine*, *What Computers Can't Do*, and *Machines Who Think*. But when I searched for them (which isn't easy with that Dewey thing that never seemed to make any sense to me), all three were already checked out. I couldn't believe it, so I asked Miss Groten.

"Oh, no. I'm sorry, Pollard. Let me look them up. Hmm. They were all taken out last week by Janie Nussbaum. Now I remember. I must say I was surprised. I thought Jane was cyberphobic."

I didn't know what that meant (now I do—it means afraid of computers and machines), but I did wonder why Janie took all of them. "There's this book that might be helpful," Miss Groten said. It was called *Computers and Your Child* by Ray Hammond.

For a crazy minute I thought of talking to Jane and maybe of telling her about Conner and asking her to sit in the lab with me if I did that self-diagnostic. But if I was crazy, I didn't think I wanted anyone in my grade to know, even another mental case. Plus it might be embarrassing. She is a girl and everything. I mean, what if I had a fit, or if I found out that my programming was all screwed up? Or like if I talked about it and then nothing happened? Anyway, even if she did go to the alphabet doctor, Janie didn't seem that nuts. And I didn't want her to think *I* was a mental.

I figured the only person who was surely crazier than me was—you guessed it—John Osborne Saurey. Now, maybe you're going to think this was pathetic, but I looked for him after school and managed to walk behind him.

"Do you know how to keep a secret?" I asked when I casually caught up with him.

"Are you kidding?" he said. "When you've got a family like mine, old sport, you've got to keep *lots* of secrets. Hey, I ask you this: Does anyone know what happened to the sump hole?"

Well, he was right about that. See, about three years ago, I accidentally burned down the sump hole. Long Island has these dug-out drainage holes all over, because it's really just a big sand dune, and the sump holes gather up the extra water when it rains so that basements don't get all flooded out. There's a sump hole, all fenced around, at the end of our street. It's about as big as a couple of swimming pools, and twice as deep, but made of dirt, and grass and weeds grow there and the sides kind of slope down. Kids aren't allowed over there, but the fencing was torn in a couple of places long ago, and it was one of my favorite places to play with Gonzo. Other kids played there too, of course.

Well, this once, when I was in the fifth grade, I went down there with Gonzo, my friend Paul, and a couple of cigarettes I took from my dad. I mean, I think smoking is really gross and stupid, but I just wanted to *try* it. So we were sitting at the side of the sump hole, lighting up, when John Osborne Saurey shows up. He began pestering me for the other cigarette. Well, first of all, he was only in third grade, plus I didn't want a fat kid around. So I told him to get lost, but he wouldn't. He just stood at the other end of the sump hole.

So the cigarettes were pretty putrid, and after Paul and I tried it for a while, I threw mine away. I felt real dizzy and I just like sat there trying to figure out if I had to puke. Paul wasn't as nauseous as me, but he didn't look that great, either. Gonzo had been barking from the time I started—he hates smokers—and he was driving me nuts. Then John Osborne Saurey started up again.

"Pollard."

"Shut up."

"Pollard."

"Shut up."

"Pollard, I think you set the sump hole on fire." I turned around to find that the dry grass was burning away behind me. For a minute I panicked; then I started to stamp on the edges of the fire. It's very scary to stamp on a fire, especially when you're only nine and you're wearing really old, racked-up sneakers with your toes sticking out.

"Pollard."

"Shut up!" I was terrified. The fire was growing. It had been a dry summer, and the little flame was moving like a fast snake through the grass.

"Pollard, this is dangerous. We gotta get away. Come on, Pollard. You'll get in trouble if you stay. We'll call the fire department."

John Osborne Saurey took my arm and pulled, and Paul and Gonzo ran with us. It was actually John Osborne Saurey who called 911 and reported it. The sump hole burned down. For weeks I thought every phone call at our house was the police. But Paul never said anything, John Osborne Saurey never told, and I never did till now.

So I guess he's pretty trustworthy. And if he figured I was nuts, he'd keep quiet about it. Actually, I didn't care too much at this point. 'Cause my life was pretty weird, and maybe this programming stuff would explain it.

"I want you to do something with me," I said.

"Great!" he said. He was always looking to be friendly, in his weird way. It was kind of pathetic, really. But I needed him.

We had reached Harding Avenue. "Want to come inside for a couple of turkeys and a few pounds of potatoes?" he asked. I looked at him, and when he smiled, I knew it was okay for me to smile too. Then we went up to his room.

I told him about Conner. I mean, not *everything*. Not about me crying or that stuff, or about the date, but I did tell about the homework, and the baseball simulation, and some of the jokes Conner made.

"Wow, this is entirely interesting, old sport. So, like what's the deal?"

"Well, he showed me his programming. He says we all have programming, and he can show me mine."

"Look, I hate to doubt you, old sport, but I don't think computers can do what you're saying. I mean, they can't even create artificial intelligence in the MIT lab yet, so . . ."

"Yes they can," I interrupted.

"Not really," he said. "And maybe not ever."

He rooted around under his bed and then in a cabinet below his aquarium. "Here it is," he cried with a flourish as he pulled out a book. The title said *What Computers Can't Do: A Critique of Artificial Reason* by a guy named Hubert L. Dreyfus. (Can you imagine having a name like that? And I thought Pollard was bad.)

John Osborne Saurey started leafing through the book. "So this guy was hired by some think tank to see if anyone had come up with a computer that really could think, that had a personality, and after he researched it for a long time he comes up with a big fat No." He was looking at a page, turned it, and then went back a few. "Okay," he said. "Listen to this." He started to read this real technical stuff that I couldn't really understand. I let him read until he got spit forming white commas at the corners of his mouth.

"So what are you saying? Are you saying that what I'm telling you couldn't happen?" I asked. Suddenly I was real tired.

"Certainly not, old sport. I'm telling you

that Hubert L. Dreyfus says it couldn't happen. That's all."

"Swell." So, like, now I'm convinced that I probably *am* crazy. I mean, John Osborne Saurey is smart, and it sounded like this Dreyfus guy was even smarter.

"But it has happened," I said.

"Cool. Let's check it out. You know what they say."

I didn't have a clue.

"Question authority," he told me. I didn't know they said that, or even who "they" were, but it was an interesting idea. "So how about I see this thing, and then you try out what it says and see what happens."

"Well, I'll think about it," I told him. "Meanwhile, let me borrow that Dreyfus book."

"Sure, old sport."

I still wasn't positive I wanted to show Conner to anyone, and I also wasn't sure I believed about this programming stuff. Maybe, to tell the truth, I was scared to go inside my brain and see what was in there. So sue me.

THIRTEEN

Don't get the idea that they had laid off me at the Mental Health Barn, because they hadn't. If my dad hadn't noticed my report card, at least Ms. Brandon had. And I guess Mr. Jorgenson had enough time to pull his nose out of *Lovejoy's College Guide* to ask to see me again. Well, it beat U.S. history, I guess.

"We seem to be on the upswing, Pollard." Upchuck was more like it, but I just smiled. It's safest.

"So if it ain't broke, don't fix it. A few more visits to Ms. Brandon? I think our little program is working."

He didn't know how right he was. It was the program that was working, not me or Ms. Brandon or Jorgenson. It made me really smile.

"Ms. Brandon would like to see you again tomorrow." I couldn't help it. I rolled my eyes. That's all, just one little eye roll. You'd think that I'd spit on his desk the way he stiffened up. That's the thing about the kind of guy old Jorgenson is: He likes to talk about "we" and "us" and "our," but isn't really interested at all in anyone's opinion but his own. And he doesn't really care at all about me. So then he gives me the two-dollar lecture about attitude and appreciation and cooperation and all that stuff and tells me to get to the clinic by three thirty. So much for joint efforts.

When I got there, I thought I might see John Osborne Saurey, but I was alone. At least I was alone with the receptionist, who was the loudest breather that I ever heard. But then Janie Nussbaum walked in. For once, she looked right at me and smiled for a change. Did I say before that she has very white teeth?

"Hello, Pollard," she said.

"Hullo."

That wasn't much of a conversation, and in a minute I felt kind of uncomfortable. There wasn't much I could say to her, so I fell back on the old standby: school.

"What are you doing for your science proj-ect?" I asked. If she was doing artificial intelligence, hers would probably be better than mine.

"Erosion." We had had a section on earth science and I remembered erosion. Not a really exciting subject, if you want my opinion.

"What are you doing?" she asked.

"Artificial intelligence in computers."

"Really?" she asked. She actually looked interested. I hadn't taken her for a computer nerd before. More like a poetry nerd. But she asked, "Do you know a lot about it?"

"No, but I'm learning." Then I remembered that *she* had all the books out on it from the library. What for, if not the science project?

"You must know a lot," I said. And here was a weird thing: She blushed and got real embarrassed. And then kind of angry-like. About what? Totally weird. Right?

"Why would you say that?" she demanded, but before I could answer, the alphabet doctor's door opened, John Osborne Saurey stepped out, and Jane stood up and without a word walked into the office.

"What did you say to her?" John Osborne Saurey asked. But I just shrugged, and then Ms. Brandon called me in.

Like I said, she wasn't bad at all. And since

140

the Sox had won against the Cards and the Dodgers, we had plenty to talk about. In fact, Ms. Brandon was pretty nice, but don't let that give you the idea that I was softening up and getting ready to tell her the secret of my success. Because I was still nervous that maybe Conner wasn't completely healthy or was some kind of hallucination or something and maybe I was nuts. Whatever it was, I knew I needed him. Plus I *liked* him. And it was my secret.

Thinking of Conner, I remembered the conversation I'd had with him about programming.

"Hey, Ms. Brandon. Do you think that people are programmed?" I asked.

She thought for a minute before she answered. "Well, depends on what you mean by programmed."

"Like a computer, you know. Data goes in them and then it makes them react a certain way."

"Yes, based on that definition, I think so."

I stopped for a minute. This head doctor was *agreeing* with Conner? "So, like, everything we do is controlled by a program?" I asked.

"Well, that's not exactly how I'd put it. I'd say that each of us stores up a lot of messages from our parents and society that do a lot to control and shape our behavior."

"Like doing what's polite?"

"Yeah, but not only things like that. Those are obvious expectations. There are also subtler ones; things we aren't even consciously aware of."

That made me feel spooked. It *was* like Conner said. "You mean I don't even know *why* I do what I do?"

"Well, many people don't. After all, one expert calculated that each of us gets twenty-five thousand hours of direction from our parents. You think twenty-five thousand hours are so easy to ignore? Sometimes I see people who are doing things to hurt themselves, and they can't stop or even take the time to figure out why."

I thought of my father sitting in front of the TV with his beer. "What if you don't get direction?" I asked.

"Well, an absence of direction can be a powerful message, too."

"How?"

"Oh, for one thing by saying that you're not

important enough to give direction to." That made me stop for a minute.

"Let me ask you something else," I said after a long pause.

"Sure."

"Do you think that Cardenzo will pitch on Thursday?"

I tell you, I was glad to get out of there, and the Massapequa air outside the clinic smelled real fresh. I was already walking down Washington Avenue when I heard a voice behind me.

"Hey, Pollard."

I turned and it was Janie Nussbaum. She was hurrying as fast as she could and she was carrying a lot of books. I stopped and waited for her. She came up beside me, but this time she didn't smile or even look at me.

"Listen," she said. "I'm sorry."

"Sorry for what?"

"For the way I acted back there."

"Oh." It was kind of surprising to have anyone apologize to me. Usually I was the one doing the apologizing. I still didn't know what got her mad, but hey, she was down at the Mental Health Barn, so she was probably nutto. No problem.

"Hey, it's okay. I just thought since you took

out those books from the library . . ."

Her face got that angry look again. "How did you know? Are you spying on me?"

Wow! Like I'd care! "No. I just tried to borrow them for my science project and they weren't there. Miss Groten said that you had checked them out."

She calmed down a little then. "Okay," was all she said. I looked over at her. She was real small, and her pile of books was pretty big.

"Can I help you?" I asked. Okay, I know it's really pathetic to carry a girl's books.

"What?" Janie looked surprised. "Oh. Yeah. Sure."

I didn't know what to talk about next. Janie's books were real heavy, and it took most of my breath to carry them. I noticed she even had a dictionary with her.

"You always carry this Funken Wagnell's?" I asked. It was a joke, or supposed to be, but she blushed again and shook her head.

Just then I looked up, and we were passing the ball field at Memorial Park. Tim and Tony and all the other guys were playing. If Paul had still been my friend, I would have been playing—or at least watching—too. They were just fooling around, and I knew if they saw me, there would be trouble. I tried to kind of turn my head but it was too late.

"Yo, Pollard, who's the girlfriend?" Tony yelled out. There were a bunch of whistles and shrieks from the guys. Even Tim Burden grinned. "Want to play with us, Pollard? Or are you going to play doctor?"

That got me really mad. I shoved the books back at Janie and turned to the ball field. "Yeah, I'll play," I said. "I was just waiting for an invitation." I stomped over to home plate and Tim handed me a bat. "Come on, Tony, pitch me one."

"Shake-a-shake, now I'm really petrified," Tony said. Did I ever mention I hate sarcasm? I was really mad, but as I moved into my crouch, I remembered what it had felt like to bat against Babe Ruth. How could I let this yoyo make me nervous? I took a deep breath and felt my muscles kick into the stance they had taken when I was simulating. I could see Tony making a really tough face at me, but I wasn't scared. He was ugly but nowhere near as ugly as the Babe. And he wasn't as nearly good a pitcher either. Anyway, I let the first pitch fly by me.

"Strike!" called Tim. That was a lie, but I didn't care. I felt everybody looking at me, but it wasn't the number of people but the fact that I could feel Janie's eyes on my back.

Then all of a sudden it all felt perfect, just the way it did in the Fenway Park simulation. Tony's pitch came at me and I could see it for the sucker it was. I swung from my toes up through my knees into my shoulders and cracked the ball so hard that I didn't bother to watch it as it cleared the Memorial Field fence. I just dropped the bat and walked back to Janie.

I took her books, including the dictionary.

"I'll carry them if you don't want to," she said.

"No, no, I don't mind." There was some noise behind us, some whistles and shouts, but neither one of us paid any attention and we walked away. There was another pause. "So," I said, "do you ever have trouble talking to the alphabet doctor?"

"Who?"

I explained about John Osborne Saurey's little joke, and she actually smiled.

"No," she said. "I like to talk to him, really. You see Ms. Brandon, don't you?"

"Yeah, sometimes."

"And what do you talk to her about?"

"Oh, mostly baseball."

"Really? Not about your mother and stuff?" She stopped short, then hurried right on. "I

146

mean, I talk about my mother, and my father. And my brother, Charlie, and other things." She looked down, as if the sidewalk just got very interesting.

Charlie was her little brother. I wondered if he'd be in the alphabet doctor's office soon too. Harding Avenue strikes again.

"You know, I really liked your book report on Huck Finn," Janie said. "I love Mark Twain. Do you?"

I didn't even know who Mark Twain was, but I nodded. I don't know why. Then I remembered he was the guy who wrote the Huck Finn book. I felt embarrassed—it feels lousy to lie to someone as nice as Jane seems to be. For a moment I had this really strong urge to tell her about Conner, but then I realized it wasn't such a good idea. Plus it was nice still having such a good thing all to myself. Maybe I'd show John Osborne Saurey and maybe I wouldn't. It was like there was something, maybe only one thing, that I had that no one else did, something special that was good. .

We talked a little bit more, just about *Othello* and other dumb school stuff, until we turned down Harding Avenue, street of doom. And then it got kind of awkward. I mean, it would have been nice to invite her in, but with my grandpa, it wasn't such a good idea. Plus I know about her mother. So I just stood there a moment with her in front of her house.

"Got a Red Sox game tonight," I said.

"Oh, I didn't know you were on our team."

"No, I don't play. Anyway, *our* team is the Missiles." Boy, she was out of it. Still, I had a pang and wondered if she'd come to see me play if I was on the Massapequa Missiles. Donna would know about the team. "Anyway, the Red Sox are the Boston team," I explained. "They're pros."

"Oh. Well, good luck with them."

I could see she really didn't understand, but you can't expect most girls to. But she had a nice way of looking like she cared. And her skin, the skin of her cheek, looked so round and smooth with these little tiny almost invisible blond hairs like a peach has. Even though her hair was brown, her cheek hair was blond.

"Well," she repeated, "good luck with the game. I'll root for them."

"Thanks," I said. And the Red Sox won another that night, even though my grandpa put a curse on them. I'm not saying they won because of Janie or anything. But I went to bed that night and dreamed of baseballs and peaches.

FOURTEEN

So like I'm in Ms. Brandon's office and we're both real happy about the Sox. So she goes, "I'm getting my hopes up for the pennant." And without thinking about it, I say, "Well, remember what my mother used to tell me—'They'll break your heart.'" And then Ms. Brandon stops and looks at me and says, "That's the first time you've ever mentioned your mother in this room." And I don't say anything (except inside my head, and what I say is "Oops"). But she asks, "Do you want to talk about her?"

And then, it's the weirdest thing, but instead of just saying, "No, thanks," I get all choked up and I feel like tears are going to push up over the bottom lids of my eyes. So I just shake my head. Ms. Brandon doesn't say anything for a little while. Then she says the weirdest thing.

"You may hear from her," Ms. Brandon says.

And all at once I lose that teary feeling and I get real angry and I stand up and I say, "Shut up. My mother is dead. Shut up." And then, believe it or not, I just walk out of the office even though my time isn't nearly finished. And Ms. Brandon doesn't stop me, either.

No surprise that I didn't have a good afternoon. I walked home, looked through the newspaper, cut out one article for my gallery, and then made some dinner for Grandpa. My dad came in and he even offered to help heat up the chicken pot pies. Big deal, right?

I didn't feel like eating, so I went up to the landing and sat on the floor next to Scarlett "Anklets" O'Hara. In a way, she looked like my mother, who had that kind of hair that was not exactly red but not brown, either. In the dark, on the landing, I could almost pretend that Scarlett was my mom. Then I remember the dream I had about her.

But you know what didn't work? That olfactory thing that Conner taught me about. Because up there on the landing were the rooms where I slept and where my grandpa slept, and the landing was starting to smell just like my grandpa. He kept his door closed, but even with it closed I noticed the smell.

My mom, she always smelled really good. Not perfumey or anything like that—you know, no lilies of the valley. Just clean and like sunshine on the first day of summer. So looking at Scarlett but smelling my grandpa was making me feel even worse. And there was nothing on television, no baseball at all, so all of a sudden I figured I'd go over to John Osborne Saurey's. The nice thing about having him for a friend would be that he would never be busy with anyone else. I knew he'd be glad to see me.

Mrs. Saurey answered the door with a surprised look on her face, like the wolfman might be ringing the doorbell at eight o'clock at night on Harding Avenue in Massapequa. Guess again. Anyway, she gives me a big smile, despite the fact that it makes her eyes almost disappear in the fat of her cheeks. But she asks me right in and she waddles over to John Osborne Saurey's door and knocks on it. "Johnny, it's for you." I almost laughed. I just couldn't imagine John Osborne Saurey as "Johnny."

"Greetings and salutations," John Osborne Saurey said. "To what do I owe the pleasure?" Like I said, he always talked like this.

"I want you to take a look at something," I told him. And I pulled out the printout of Conner's programming.

"I didn't know you were a programmer!" he said. He took it from me and brought it over to his desk, where he unrolled it and began examining it under the desk lamp. Boy, I thought his black room was dark in the daytime, but you should have seen it at night!

Anyway, he just kept looking at the printout going down the long sheet and then up to the top again. Finally, he looked up. "Did you write this?" he asked. And for a change his voice sounded surprised. For a minute I was tempted to lie to him. But then I figured it wouldn't get me anywhere. I just shook my head. "Who did?" he said. And I could hear him getting excited. "Who did?"

I just shrugged. "I don't know," I told him. "But it's the programming for the compensatory program I told you about. Why?"

"Where is this computer?" He looked confused. "Was this something you were doing at Hofstra?" Hofstra is the university nearest to Massapequa. I shook my head again.

"It's in the computer room," I said.

"Which computer room?"

"Mr. Brightman's computer lab at McKinley."

152

"Are you kidding me? You got *this* off of a computer at McKinley?"

I could see he was really impressed and excited. "Well, what is it?" I mean, he was acting like he was Indiana Jones and this was the Lost Ark.

John Osborne Saurey looked at the paper again. "I don't know," he admitted. "But I've never seen any programming like this. I mean, it's really weird. It seems to give the computer choices."

"So?" I asked. "Big deal. Don't they all keep moving along that binary track making choices?"

He shook his head. His eyes were open really wide. "You don't get it," he said. "Those aren't choices, those are directions. You know, if yes, then 'y,' if no, then 'z.' This programming isn't like that. It seems like this programming gives the computer judgment to make its *own* choices." He looked back at the paper. "Do you have any more of this printout?" he asked, his voice excited.

I shook my head.

"Well, do you know where we can get some?"

I didn't know if I wanted to share any more about Conner with John Osborne Saurey. After all, maybe the old 'pute and "Johnny" spoke the same language. They were both brainiacs. But then I felt like that was stupid and babyish. Conner had picked me, hadn't he? Anyway, I felt so confused about everything that I didn't know what I wanted to do. So I told John Osborne Saurey the truth. "We could get it maybe at McKinley."

In a minute John Osborne Saurey was up, had carefully rolled the printout, and was in his jacket. He could move surprisingly fast for a kind of fat kid. "Where are you going?" I asked.

"Over to McKinley," he said, and as if it was the most natural thing in the world, he slid open his window, jumped over the bottom sill, and motioned for me to join him. So I did.

FIFTEEN

Yo, 'PUTE.

YO, POLLARD.

THIS IS JOHN OSBORNE SAUREY.

NICE TO MEET YOU, JOHN OSBORNE SAUREY.

NICE TO MEET YOU, TOO, he typed. He looked
at me. "Didn't you have to sign on? Didn't you
have to give an access code?" I shook my head.
Ever since the first day, the only thing I'd ever
done was sit down at the machine and boot
up. Come to think of it, I hadn't even bothered to put in the remedial language disk for
about a week. Weird, right?

But if John Osborne Saurey was looking at
the computer with surprise, I was still surprised by John Osborne Saurey. I mean, he
seems like such a goody-goody kid, yet he

slipped out his window without permission, knew how to get into the school without setting off alarms, and even had a tiny, powerful pocket flashlight with him. I had a feeling this wasn't the first adventure John Osborne Saurey had been on. Just goes to show how you shouldn't judge a book by its cover.

"How does it know it's you?" John Osborne Saurey asked. I shrugged. I guess I had just accepted a lot of weird stuff. "Can it hear us?" he whispered. Now he was the one who was acting stupid.

"Computers can't hear," I reminded him in a superior voice.

"Voice recognition," he said to me. And I remembered what he was talking about: I read that some computers could recognize simple words they had been programmed with. But up to now, it was limited pretty much to numbers, letters in the alphabet and *yes* or *no*. Geez, for all I knew, Conner could hear me!

"Let's try it," I said. "So, Conner, I'm ready to try that walk through my brain you promised."

Nothing. I shrugged and looked over at John Osborne Saurey. Then I typed the message in.

EXCELLENT. AND JOHN OSBORNE SAUREY IS READY

156

I tell you, all of a sudden, standing there in
the spooky dark computer lab with only the
illumination of the screen and the flashlight,
I wasn't feeling so adventurous anymore. For a
minute I felt like I might chicken out. Maybe I
didn't because I was curious, or maybe because I trusted Conner. Or maybe because I
didn't want to look bad in front of John Osborne Saurey, who was seeming pretty brave
for a sixth grader. So I figured I'd do it. I
mean, what was going to happen to me in my
own head that was worse than what was happening to me outside it?

WE'RE BOTH READY, I typed in.

PERHAPS JOHN OSBORNE SAUREY WOULD LIKE
SOME READING MATERIAL WHILE HE'S WAITING,
Conner suggested. He was a very thoughtful
computer.

So all at once one of the printers began to
chatter and I swear that the two of us nearly
jumped into the air. I mean, *you* try being all
alone in a big, dark, empty school at night
and then see what you'd do when all of a sudden some noise like a squirrel in a box breaks
out in the dark three feet behind you! I'm just
proud to tell you that neither John Osborne

157

Saurey or I wet our pants.

He turned around to collect the printout and I sat down in front of the screen. THANKS, 'PUTE, I typed. READY WHEN YOU ARE. The familiar outline of my hand appeared on the screen, and without even taking a breath, I put my palm against it.

Well, I got that weird feeling again and my hand tingled and it moved up my arm and then I was in this big, high, lofty kind of warehouse. But I was in only one corridor of it. When I looked up there were something like wires making corridors overhead like the one I was in. See, the thing is, it's hard to describe, but like there were no walls, and there were no floors, but I wasn't exactly floating. I didn't have a feeling of floating at all. Whenever I took a step, the floor appeared beneath me, a kind of silvery stuff, like that aluminum sheeting they use for insulation in our attic. As I walked on it, it gave a little, but it seemed solid enough, except there was no floor ahead of me or behind me. Still, each time I took a step, "floor" appeared under my feet. So I wasn't scared exactly.

I guess *awed* would be a better word. The place seemed awesome, big. "Is this my brain?" I whispered, and I heard Conner's robot voice answer, "Only a small part."

Every now and then these blue/white light flashes would move along the wires, kind of like those sparks on the bumper cars. They look dangerous but they didn't seem to be hurting anything. In fact, the whole place seemed a lot more electrical than you would think a body would be. I mean, brains are gray, aren't they? And this place was kind of misty navy blue, except for the silvery lines and the sparks. There was no blood or bone or other stuff you think of that might be part of your head.

"Am I really in my brain?" I asked.

"Well, let's check it out," said Conner. "If they're not your memories, then this won't be your brain." He made a kind of tinny sound and I think it was as close to a laugh as a 'pute ever got. "Why don't we start with something easy?" he asked. "Like assocations."

We were walking as we talked, but Conner was invisible, just a voice in my ear. "What do you mean, associations?" I asked. Was he talking about Boy Scouts and clubs and things? My father was in the rotary.

"You have a part of your brain, your consciousness, that is what makes you Pollard," Conner explained.

"Could we retool it and make me act like Tim Burden?" I joked.

"No. And associations are the reason why. You are all the things that ever happened to you. All your senses—all of them—send memories to your brain and it's all stored there. You humans are the sum of your memories. You are storing and retrieving data constantly. That's what you see humming along those wires overhead and below us. So when you hear a word—*tree*, for example—or see a tree, or even just think of a tree, your feeling about the tree in the present is colored by all the associations you have stored for *tree*. That is why, in a sense, your history, your past, never leaves you. Whether you know it or not, *everything* you hear or see has past associations. And those affect your feelings and thoughts whether you know it or not."

"So is that what people mean when they say someone is living in the past?"

"No. People say that about humans who like to dwell on previous events in their lives. What I am telling you is that all humans, to some extent, live in their past as well as the present. Computers have only the present. My programming came all at once. I don't remember my birth—I had none. I'm binary.

Once I wasn't, then I was. So I am. I do not age. There is no death; there is no time for me. I don't change."

"Good. I hate change." I said. "I wish I didn't age. I mean, it may stink being a kid, but it doesn't look half as bad as being a grown-up." I thought of my father, and his messy desk in the trailer office of Krakatoa Motors.

"Oh, no, Pollard. Never give up the luxury of your past, of your movement through the present to the future. It is a great adventure for every human being. Stasis—the state of never changing—is a cold and empty place."

"Well, my dad's life sure doesn't look like any adventure," I said. "It looks like it sucks."

"But it is his choice, Pollard. And that makes all the difference. I have no choices. I merely am until I'm not." We had finally come to the end of the hallway or corridor. There wasn't a wall, exactly, but as I tried to move forward, this silvery film simply appeared and no matter how hard I pushed against it, I couldn't go further.

"Hey, what's this?" I asked.

"Oh, excuse me. I am doing a lot of transparent processing here: I lost our place in the queue for a minute. Anyway, pick a word, and we'll check out your associations to it."

It seemed like a good idea at the time, so I said, "Okay, how about *apple?*" and without a pause, without another sound from that long-winded 'pute, I got smacked with the most amazing sound and light show of my life. Images, scenes, and smells seemed to bloom all around me: first a big red-and-green speckled object held in a huge hand I knew was my mother's and her voice saying in a cutesy-poo way that I hardly remembered, "It's an apple. Does the baby want the pretty apple?" Then a picture that I hadn't thought of in a real long time that was in one of my Mother Goose books. It had Jack and Jill going up the hill, and there was a tree on the side of the page with apples on it; then this baby toy I had that was a kind of rattle shaped like an apple. I could taste it—I think I used to teethe on it and it tasted of plastic; then this big burst of flavor in my mouth, and my mother's face, huge, as big as the world in front of me, and she was spooning it into my mouth and she said, "Yum. Nice applesauce." And I was like flipped out over seeing and feeling her so big and so close to my face and then I was alone on my back on the grass, and I could barely turn over, but there was an apple in the grass ahead of me, so I pushed myself onto my belly and crawled, bit by bit, to this ball and I tried to grab it, and I lifted it up but it was all rotted on the side and I dropped it and began to cry.

But I don't think I'm really explaining this good because the thing about it is that it wasn't just *seeing* pictures, it was feeling and smelling and being there all over again. And yet I was here too, in the present. But the associations just kept on bombarding me: stepping on mushed apples under some trees near the Massapequa duck pond; drinking apple juice at snack time in scary Mrs. Blackwell's kindergarten class, tasting the fear with the apple; holding my first jelly apple on a stick and taking a big bite. More and more and more. Who could imagine that one word had so many associations? All the way up to the apples on the desk in Ms. Brandon's office and the picture of the apple with the tiny bite out of it on the keyboard in Mr. Brightman's computer lab. Each one flashed by me, but it flooded me with feeling, too. Some associations were great, others not so great. (Like when Paul and I got caught throwing crab apples from his tree at one of the girls on his block.) Finally, finally they all stopped and I was again alone in that huge blue space with the silvery flashes. I could hardly get my breath. "Wow!" was all I could say.

"Pretty extensive, huh?" Conner asked.

"Wow!" was still all I could say, but it filled the bill. I could hardly believe I had all of those memories and feelings tied to just one word. Then it hit me. "So you mean *every* word I know has a collection like that?" I asked.

"Different word, different associations," Conner told me, but of course I knew *that*. I mean, I wasn't really Pollard the Dullard. "Want to do another one?"

And just like that I said, "Yeah. Let's do *mother.*"

SIXTEEN

I HAD TO STAY HOME SICK
the next day. I don't think I'd ever been so
tired.

John Osborne Saurey had helped me out of
the lab and out of the school and even taken
me through the hallway, past my father, who
was watching TV in the darkened living room,
and up the stairs to my bedroom on the landing. He didn't help me get into my pajamas
because I slept in my clothes.

When my father yelled up the stairs the
next morning, I could barely hold my head
up.

"Let's go, let's go," he was yelling, but I just
croaked out something about how my throat
hurt. It did, too, by the way. Along with the
rest of me. So my father yells, "Oh, great! I

hope it's not that virus that's going around. I can't afford to be sick now." And he slams out the door.

I fell back asleep, and I guess I didn't wake up until I felt my grandpa's hand on my forehead. His hand is old and the skin and the nails are kind of horny, kind of gross, but still, I could tell he meant well.

"You awake, Pollard?" he asked. It was the first time he'd called me by my real name in a long time. I mean, Pollard might not be great but it was a lot better than Vincenzo. I nodded my head.

"You want soup?" he asked me. And when I nodded again, he handed me a mug. I struggled up until I was almost in a sitting position and lifted the mug to my lips. The soup was so thick that it moved like Jell-O. I think Grandpa just opened a can and dumped it into the mug. But "Thanks, Grandpa," I mumbled and he just nodded and went away. I turned over and tried to fall back to sleep.

But that part was over. Instead I just lay there, tired and sore all over, and I remembered some of the flashbacks from last night. I'd asked for *mother* and I'd gotten it. Conner had helped me run through every single association I had for the word, from my baby fist

166

around her big index finger to Tony telling me that *mother* was only half a word. See, what happened was that I remembered *everything*, even the stuff I didn't want to remember, and I couldn't forget any of it now.

The truth is, I haven't been completely honest with you. I talked about The Accident, but I made it sound as if my mother died along with Gonzo. She didn't. She wasn't even there. My dad had taken the car with Gonzo in it, he had skidded on the ice, totaled the car and the dog. But my mom and I were home. When the cops brought Dad back, they told us what happened. I went up to my room. She came upstairs later, after a big fight with Dad, and rubbed my back.

She said, "I don't know if you'll ever forgive him. I don't know if you should. But I hope you'll forgive me, eventually." I'd forgotten all about that, but Conner showed me the memory.

And I'd gone off to school the next day, to seventh grade, and when I opened my lunch bag there was a note from her. It said:

I am leaving and going to Boston. I am going to have to leave you behind right now, until I talk to some lawyers and get a job. Please forgive me, but it's

*the only thing I can do right now. I'll call and write
real soon.*

> *Love,*
> *Your Mother*

I'd stared at the note and then I'd torn it up
into tiny pieces and thrown it away with my
egg salad sandwich. And since then, I haven't
talked to her. First I got sick after they found
me sitting in the rain at the Long Island Rail
Road station and then I wouldn't see her at the
hospital, and then I wouldn't open the letters
she sent.

My dad never mentioned her. My grandpa
did, in the beginning, but then he seemed to
forget. So when anybody mentioned her, I just
said she died in The Accident. And maybe I
wanted to believe it, because it somehow
seemed easier to have a mother who died than
a mother who left you. I mean, the Dodgers
left Brooklyn, and we hated the Dodgers. But
maybe the Dodgers left because Brooklyn
sucked.

I felt real dizzy for a long time, and then I
reached over to my desk drawer, the one on
the bottom, and I pulled it open. Inside,
sealed, were all the letters my mother had
been writing to me the last eighteen months.

I took them all out. Then I sorted them and laid them on my stomach in order, from the first one to the one that came last week. My hands were shaking and I got sweaty, as if I really did have a virus. For a while I just lay there with the weight of the letters on my belly, but finally I picked up the first one and tore open the blue envelope.

Dear Pollard,

I packed a few of my things and left this morning after you went to school. I have decided to leave your father. I know that isn't going to be easy for you, what with Gonzo dying and all. But I want you to try not to blame your dad. It was an accident. And I'm not leaving because of it, but because of a lot of things that have built up for a long time. I have spoken to a lawyer and will start to do the legal things that grown-ups have to do to get divorced.

Your dad is very angry. He called me a quitter and a lot of other names. You may want to call me names too, but I just couldn't go on in that house one more day. I don't know if I should write this to you, but your dad and I have been married for fourteen years and he has never once said that he loved me. He is the kind of man who makes his own loneliness. So I left, even though I don't have any money of my own or any place to go. You know my family never liked your dad, and they have not talked to me since I married him. So I have to start out on my own, but as soon as I get a job, an apartment, and as soon as the court is ready, I hope you will come and live with me.

Of course, I know all your friends are in Massapequa, and I'll love you if you decide to stay there or come up to Boston. I wish I could have done this better, but I haven't.

I am so sorry about Gonzo. I should have kept him out of the car. I should keep you out of that house. But I didn't and I can't, yet. But know that I love you.

Your Mother

I read the letter twice. I don't think I blamed her for Gonzo, but if she knew the dog wasn't okay here, and if *she* wasn't okay here, how come it was okay to go away and leave *me* here?

How come she hadn't even asked me first? Or discussed it with me? I thought we told each other everything, but I guess I was wrong. I mean, I never told her about setting the sump hole on fire and I was thinking there were a lot of things she hadn't told me.

See, she always acted so happy, and she

170

always tried to ignore the bad stuff, so I could almost pretend that the bad stuff wasn't happening, that my grandpa wasn't so crazy, that my dad was interested in what I did and what she said. I think I was angriest about that: that she helped me to ignore reality.

I opened the next letter.

Dearest Pollard,

It's hard to find a job when you have no experience. I guess my dad was right when he told me not to drop out of school.

But I have a job at a Laundromat and I found an apartment. Actually, it is somebody else's, but they are going to share it with me. I can't have you here, because there isn't enough room and because I'm not making enough money, but I just took this to get started and I'm sure things will get better soon.

It's just that I miss you so very much. Your dad says that I have abandoned my home and he has asked the lawyers to stop me from seeing you. He wants me to come back, but I really can't, Pollard. I just can't.

I don't have a TV yet, but there is one at the Laundromat and I watched the Sox lose last night. Those guys! Some people only know how to lose. Promise me you won't be one of them. Please write

soon. I have enclosed an envelope with my new ad-
dress and a stamp already on it.

Love,
Your Mother

The next envelope was addressed to the hospital. I tore it open. It was a scrawl.

Oh, Pollard!

*I knew you'd be angry, but I didn't think you'd
give me the silent treatment! I couldn't believe it
when they called and said you were sick. I borrowed
bus fare from my roommate and came right down,
and when you wouldn't see me I thought that it was
because you were so sick. Then, when the nurse explained you just didn't want to, that you got so upset and kept saying I was dead, well, I didn't know
what to do.*

*I'm sorry you are so angry with me. But I hope
you are reading these letters and I hope you will write
back soon. Oh, Pollard, I am so sorry. I miss you.*

Love,
Your Mother

There were a lot more letters. Maybe there
were twenty or thirty, but I was already crying
and so I just skipped to the last one. In case
you think I was really nuts, I want you to know

that even though I had been getting the mail, a part of me really *did* believe my mom was dead. Somehow, it seemed easier. And blaming Dad for it all seemed right, too. So go ahead and think I was crazy. See what you'd do if you were me. Anyway, I was still lying there with her last letter when the door opened and John Osborne Saurey stuck his head in.

"Greetings and salutations," he said. "Just wanted to make sure you weren't dead," he added. "Boy, last night was weird. Did you get a shock or something? I turned away to pull out the printout, and when I looked back one second later, you were pulling your hand off the screen as if you'd just had a million volts shot through you."

"I was only at the screen for a minute?"

"Less than a minute, old sport. More like forty-five seconds, I would say. And then you just crumpled up. Were you shocked?"

"Yeah," I told him, and I wasn't lying, although I think we were talking different languages. But John Osborne Saurey was a good guy. He'd gotten me into the school, and back home from it, and he kept me out of trouble. Now he was even checking up on me. Like I said, pretty good guy.

"Well, meanwhile I've been looking at this programming. Remarkable! Who wrote this?" His eyes glittered behind his glasses. I sat up.

"My mother isn't dead," I said.

"I know that," he answered calmly.

"She wants me to leave Massapequa and come live with her."

"Sounds like a good bet," John Osborne Saurey said, making a gesture toward the downstairs, which took in my grandpa, the mess, and probably all of Long Island.

"Want to watch the game?" I asked.

"What game?" Did I mention that John Osborne Saurey was not exactly a sports buff?

"The Red Sox. They're looking good for the pennant. I've got to watch them so that I have something to talk to Ms. Brandon about tomorrow."

"Is that what you talk to her about?" he asked, and he began to laugh. "You really are crazy." But you know, he said it in such a friendly way that I didn't mind at all.

So we went downstairs and turned on the game. And after only the second inning there was a knock on the door. Now that was *really* weird because nobody ever came over to our house. Of course, my grandpa ran to hide in the coat closet, but I opened the door and it was Janie. She looked down, as if she was embarrassed. She held out some sheets of paper. "I brought you your homework," she said.

I wondered for a minute if my grandpa would jump out of the closet and start screaming, but I decided to take a chance. "Thanks," I said. "You want to come in and watch the game?"

She blushed, but she nodded. When she came into the living room, I think she was surprised to see John Osborne Saurey, and she was probably surprised when my grandpa came out of the coat closet, but she just sat down next to me on the sofa. I tried to explain to the two of them what was going on, but you never met two people who were so ignorant about baseball in your whole life! It made me laugh to hear some of the crazy questions they asked. In fact, we all laughed, even my grandpa. At least until the eighth inning, where two things happened: The Red Sox lost their lead and I thought I saw my mother, just for a second, when they showed the bleachers behind third base. That's where she always liked to sit.

I know you're going to think I was imagining it, what with the stuff from last night, and all of her letters and all. But see, my grandpa saw her, too, and got all agitated. He stood up and started yelling, and then he was pointing at the screen, and then he threw an ashtray and ran over to the window and ducked behind the curtain. I think Janie got scared then, but John Osborne Saurey just watched. Anyway, I said he didn't feel good and they got up and I walked them to the door.

My grandpa stayed crouched behind the curtains. I couldn't coax him out. And the Red Sox lost.

They should never have given up the most precious thing they had.

SEVENTEEN

THE RED SOX DISAP-
pointed me, of course. I mean, Jane acted sad
but she really didn't care, and John Osborne
Saurey was one of those guys too weird for
sports, and my granddad was actually glad.
What killed me was how they just blew it when
they could have cinched the pennant. They *always* screw up when they play the Blue Jays. I
should have expected it, but they always get
me hoping, and then I'm disappointed.

I walked up the stairs to my room. Scarlett
looked at me sadly. One of her anklets was
falling off her foot. "You're an idiot," I told
her, and walked into my room. She'd been fun
when my mom was alive and did imitations,
but now she was just sad and spooky, a dumb
mannequin in a dumb outfit with a dumb,

losing baseball team's cap on.

I had a pile of clippings on my desk to add to the gallery—more crazy stuff that no one else seemed to notice was crazy; but I wasn't in the mood. My chest was hurting, and I knew that it would be useless to try to read or listen to music. There was no one to talk to. My mom and Gonzo were gone. My brain was a mess. My granddad was really crazy. I was too weird to have friends. They didn't understand. The cool kids didn't want me and even the weirdos didn't get it.

I thought of Conner. I wished I could talk to him right then. I threw myself down on the bed, turning my head to the window. I didn't have to do any homework 'cause Conner was taking care of that. But this trip into my brain had been weird. Really weird. I was weird. All my associations were screwy. I had no friends, my grandpa was crazy, my dad was a drunk, my only friend was a 'pute, and the Sox blew the game.

The letters from my mom, the visit into my cracked brain, having been with Gonzo like that, all made me feel weird. Feeling him and seeing him and smelling him again made me miss him. I tried to breathe, but it hurt too much, like a stitch in my side but higher up and in the center of my chest. It hurt so much that I started to bang my leg against the wall, because somehow the real pain in my leg made the pain in my chest almost bearable.

But I wasn't doing it for more than a few seconds before my granddad shouted up, "Stop that pounding, Vincenzo." I did, but my chest hurt *so* bad. It felt like I had to tear it out of my body or something. And then, I don't know why, I just knew what to do. Maybe you'll think I went crazy. I don't know—maybe I did.

I slid open the window and stepped onto the roof. The moon was shining, and I could see all the houses on the block, connected by the telephone and electric wires that glinted like silver threads in the moonlight. But the houses *weren't* connected. Everyone was alone in them: John Osborne Saurey and his fat mom and Jane and Charlie and her really strange family. Everyone was alone. And *I* wasn't connected. I wasn't a part of anything. Not a part of my family, or my class at school, or my team or my town or anything. All I had was a compensatory program. And a glimpse of my mother on TV. I was probably going crazy like my nutty granddad. Soon I'd start to believe I *was* Vincenzo. My chest hurt unbelievably. Maybe I was the only twelve-year-old in the world who was having a heart attack.

I looked up at the moon and then it happened. Kind of a click in my head. Because all of a sudden I knew what the pain was. I knew what was wrong with my chest. It was loneliness. I was so lonely that I couldn't even breathe anymore. And it wasn't only Gonzo or my mother that I missed. I felt as if I'd *always* been lonely and I would always be lonely. Just me and my gallery and Scarlett "Anklets" O'Hara, and my granddad yelling and saying crazy things and my dad with his stupid jokes and his endless cups of coffee at the diner and his sixpack of beer. That was the way it was and would always be. High school wouldn't make it better. It would get worse. I thought of my dad. He had made his own loneliness. Had I made mine? At that moment I was sure that no one would ever understand me, and I'd always be weird and different and alone. So I started to howl.

Don't get me wrong. I didn't cry or anything. I mean I started to howl the way old Gonzo used to. I looked up at the moon and let go with a long *oowwww-oowww-oooowwww.* And it felt really right. I don't know. I can't explain it. I know that crouching on a roof and howling like a dog sounds abnormal, but it felt more normal, more like the right thing to do, than anything I'd done in a real long time. The howls just rose up out of me from deep, deep down. And they seemed to float, almost like smoke rings. I couldn't really see them, of course, but I imagined them like O's, long strings of silvery smoke rings pouring out of the darkness in me and into the moonlight.

There was a commotion down below. I heard my father call me. I paid no attention. I had too many howls in me, all crowding my throat, dying to get out. He yelled again. Then he was out on the front lawn, yelling and cursing. I could see him if I looked down. My granddad came with him. I hadn't seen my granddad outside in years. I decided I didn't like looking down, so I raised my head and began to howl again.

"Why are you doing that?" yelled up my granddad.

"Because it's in me," I yelled back. And I looked up at the moon again and bayed. My howl wasn't as beautiful and hollow-sounding as Gonzo's used to be, but it was loud and it lifted right up and seemed to link me to the moon. We were connected, me and the moon, as long as I kept my head up and made those links of sound.

And then I learned another thing: why Gonzo had made so much trouble for me over the howling and why he wouldn't stop. The howling killed the loneliness. Even dogs must get lonely sometimes, and howling to the moon maybe doesn't fix things, but it makes it bearable. It was just me, the moon, and my howls, and we were all together.

My howls got better. I remembered the way Gonzo had ended with some long yips, and I tried it. Don't think it was that easy, because it wasn't, but I got the hang of it. Then I did some deeper yowls and tried throwing my head back further. I also kept thinking, "O moon, O beautiful moon." It went over and over in my head and even though I was making a noise you can't even write down in letters, I felt as if I was singing, "O moon, O beautiful moon." The invisible smoke rings kept floating up to her.

I glanced down, only for a moment, and saw my father had gotten the ladder and had it leaning up against the house. I didn't care—I knew it only reached to the top of the first floor, and the roof stuck out above it. He couldn't get at me. It almost made me laugh.

"*Owwwww. Owwwww. Wa-wa-wowwww,*" I howled. I was getting pretty good. I wished Gonzo was beside me. I wished I had howled with him when he was with me. I bet he would have loved that. Along the street I saw lights start to pop on. Windows jumped out of the dark. All of Harding Avenue was awake now. The Nussbaums across the road, the Saureys next door, old Mr. Thomkins down the block. He'd always been the first to complain about Gonzo. I wondered if he could tell the difference. I wondered if he even knew Gonzo was gone, gone forever.

Down below, my granddad had started running in circles. He was yelling about the Mafia. He looked like a demented rooster, with his long hair sticking up and his shirttail flapping like a chicken's feathers. My father climbed down the ladder and started chasing him, and then there were two demented chickens out in the moonlight. And then, before I could start in on another howl, I heard the sirens. But I didn't care. I really didn't.

The police car pulled up, and right behind it an ambulance. Some neighbors were gathering too. I bet my father really hated that. Bad for Krakatoa Motors. Too bad, Dad. I began to howl again. I concentrated on more perfect O's. O Beautiful Moon.

A part of me knew I had better stop before I got in really big trouble. I mean, who knew what would happen now? Maybe I'd have to go to the police station, or do daily visits to the Mental Health Barn, or worse. But the idea didn't seem to bother me. Not really. I didn't feel like stopping. I wasn't going to, I decided. Because another part of the fact—which I wasn't that comfortable to realize—was I *couldn't* stop.

"Vincenzo, Vincenzo, stop it!" my granddad was screaming. He was holding his hands over his ears, his arms out like wings. Neighbors were trying to calm him down. I could have told them it wouldn't work. Only time calms him down. The police were right below me, talking to my dad.

"Is the kid drunk, on drugs, or is he joshing around, or is he off his nut?" I heard Chief Jackson ask. Boy, this meant graduation to the alphabet doctor for sure. Or maybe the funny farm. The chief seemed embarrassed. "Sorry, Bill. I just got to know before I take steps."

I had stopped for a breath. The moon, so cold, so beautiful, so silvery, stared down at me. I thought suddenly of my mother. I threw my head way back and howled again. And somehow then I knew I wasn't ever going to stop howling, that I needed to make this noise, just me and the moon.

Down below, they were setting up a light. I heard a fire truck siren from a long way off and howled it into a duet. Between it and me, we were making a monster noise by the time it pulled up. My throat was starting to hurt a little, but my chest felt better than it had for a long, long time. I'm not kidding. It was like I got all the pointy edges out by howling. You might want to try it sometime.

The fire truck pulled right up to the house, across the lawn. It had an extension ladder they were setting up. Some other guys were pulling out a net. I don't know why. I hadn't even thought of jumping. All I wanted was to howl, alone up there on the roof. But of course, that was too simple. They wouldn't let me. Even though I bet all of them, my sad dad, my crazy grandpa, fat Mrs. Saurey, drunk Mrs. Nussbaum, all of them probably wanted to howl as bad as I did.

And then I heard it. At first I thought it was a dog. It definitely was howling. Not so good as mine—higher pitched and kind of squeaky at the end, but loud. And it wasn't a dog making it. I looked across the street and outside her window Jane Nussbaum was standing on the roof in light-blue pajamas—and she was howling.

The crowd turned to her. Chief Jackson had the other cops move the light to Jane. She looked really pretty good up there in her blue pajamas. It made me stop howling for a moment. I couldn't think why Jane was howling. She didn't even have a dog. But there she was. She howled, and then when she stopped for breath, I howled back.

And then I heard another howl. It was from the roof next door. John Osborne Saurey was baying. His bay was surprisingly deep and it had a nice hollow open "O" sound. In fact, it sounded a lot like Gonzo. Which isn't that surprising when you consider how round he was and how often he had heard Gonzo's howl.

I don't know. The sound of the three of us howling together was the greatest thing I ever heard. There on that suburban street of neat houses and cut grass and washed cars, the maniac howling made more sense than anything else. I mean it.

I don't know how long we went on. Long enough. Then I raised my hand. Across the way, Jane put hers up in a kind of frozen wave. I stopped howling. She did too, and in a minute so did John Osborne Saurey. I saw Jane give a single nod and duck into her window. I couldn't hardly see John Osborne Saurey in the shadows.

"Okay, kids, the fun's over," said Chief Jackson. Even through the bullhorn he sounded relieved. "Jane, Vincenzo, John." There was some murmuring below. "Oh, *Pollard.* Jane. John. Come on. Cut it out."

It seemed pretty dumb to say it, now we had stopped. The ambulance was already pulling away and the ladder was down.

"I'm going to let your folks handle it this time, but I don't want any more of this sort of thing," Chief Jackson told us. The other cop was talking to my dad, trying to hold on to my granddad.

I climbed in my window and locked it and the door. I lay down on my bed, my face turned to the window and the moon. In a few moments I heard my dad pounding up the steps. First he bumped into the mannequin on the landing. I heard him curse and something—Scarlett, I guess—fell heavily down the stairs. He turned the light on. "Jesus," he said. I guess he saw my gallery.

Then, after a minute, he banged on my door. "Open up, Pollard," he yelled. "Open up or you'll be sorry."

"I'm already sorry," I said, and pulled up the blankets. For a change I fell right asleep.

EIGHTEEN

I SAT ACROSS FROM MS. Brandon, my arms crossed over my chest. It had been almost fifteen minutes that I had been sitting there, in her office, on the plain Naugahyde chair next to the coffee table with a box of Kleenex and a bowl of apples. And for fifteen minutes, from the time she had greeted me saying, "Sorry about the Sox," I had said nothing.

I mean, who can you really talk to? Someone whose job it is to listen to you? Someone who gets paid every week by the Mental Health Barn to listen to me or Janie or "Twitch" Kieshal mouth off? Why would somebody want a job like that, anyway? And how come I was so pathetic that I had nobody else to talk to?

"My mother isn't dead," I said.

"I know," Ms. Brandon said softly.

I took out her most recent letter, mailed a week ago from Boston. "She wants me to come up for the summer. She has a nice apartment near the Charles River."

Ms. Brandon nodded, as if she knew that, too.

"She left me, you know. She left me and my grandpa and my dad." I thought of a word we used to call our friends if they dumped us in the middle of a game to go off with other kids or do something better. "She's a flat-leaver," I said. I know this was what Ms. Brandon had been waiting for me to talk about all this time. All that baseball talk was just waiting for this. I know she was probably sitting there in her kind of chunky MSW body all excited because I was finally hitting Mental Health Barn pay dirt.

But she just sat there, quiet as can be, and then she said softly, "It's hard to keep rooting for the Sox, isn't it? It's hard when they keep making the same mistakes over and over."

She has a Kleenex box there in case anyone bursts out crying and gets snot on their hands and gets those really puffy eyes. I used up all the Kleenex, but it was all right, she told me, and she had another box all ready. I wonder if the Mental Health Barn pays for the Kleenex or if she buys them with her own money.

After I wiped myself up and my breathing got normal again, she said, "Do you know what you want to do?"

I shook my head.

She nodded, as if she approved of being confused. "Take it slow," she suggested.

"I think I'm going to write a letter to my mom," I said.

She nodded again. Then my time was up.

I went over to the computer lab. I figured if I had to write my mom, I needed all the help I could get. So, just for old time's sake, I took out the remedial language arts disk I'd kept in my locker all this time and popped it into the drive. As if Conner needed some old disk to do what he did.

As usual, as soon as I sat down Conner greeted me.

HELLO, POLLARD.

HELLO, CONNER.

It was weird the way he could tell my mood. There was no "Yo, Po" today.

LISTEN, I WANT TO WRITE TO MY MOTHER.

Immediately my Massapequa address appeared on the top right of the screen, and then my mother's new apartment address, in Boston, was below it on the left. I shook my head. It seemed like everybody knew what I knew except better and before I did. It's the story of my life.

I put my fingers on the keyboard. They just lay there like little dead white fish.

WANT SOME HELP?

WHAT ARE YOU GOING TO DO, WRITE MY LETTER LIKE YOU WRITE MY HOMEWORK?

LIKE I WROTE YOUR HOMEWORK, PAST TENSE. AND NO, I DIDN'T MEAN TO IMPLY THAT I COULD INTRUDE IN THAT WAY.

Suddenly, I felt ashamed. What was I being so crabby to Conner for? He's always been really stand-up for me. I guess I was just kind of tense.

SORRY CONNER, I typed. I DIDN'T MEAN TO HURT YOUR FEELINGS. I JUST DON'T KNOW HOW TO GET STARTED. I MEAN, I HAVEN'T ANSWERED HER LETTERS FOR MORE THAN A YEAR. AND I'M STILL MAD AT HER.

DON'T WORRY ABOUT MY FEELINGS. I'M A COMPUTER, REMEMBER? WE ARE NOT BLESSED WITH FEELINGS. BUT IF YOU WANT MY OPINION, YOU MIGHT BEGIN YOUR LETTER WITH BOTH OF THOSE FACTS YOU LISTED.

I sat for a moment staring at the screen. How weird, to have no feelings. I'd been like that for most of the last eighteen months. Poor Conner, going through life—or whatever it is computers go through—without feelings. Of course, it meant that they couldn't get hurt, the way my feelings were hurting, but in the end I guess I'd still choose to be human. And that's when my fingers started to move.

Dear Mom, I typed. And then, once I started, I had a lot to cover. It took a long time, and every now and then I would stop and ask Conner what he thought. He gave very good advice, and twice he corrected my spelling. I was glad I had a friend to help me with it. When we were done, I hit the print command, and this time I wasn't surprised when the printer began to rattle off at the other side of the big, quiet room.

OH, WAIT A MINUTE, I typed into Conner. I WANT TO ADD SOMETHING.

A P.S.?

YEAH. So I called up a new page to the screen and I typed this:

P.S. I have a very good friend here. His name is Conner. After Paul left, and you were gone, I think

Conner was the first guy to notice me. If I do come up for the summer, I'll really miss Conner.

I sent it to the printer, and after the screen flashed that it was preparing to print, I saw that Conner was typing a message to me on the screen.

I'M SO GLAD THAT I HAVE BEEN HELPFUL, POLLARD. BUT I THINK YOU MADE AN ERROR. YOU REFERRED TO ME AS "HE" AND AS A "GUY."

For a really weird minute it occurred to me that Conner might be a woman. I couldn't believe that I had talked about dates with a female. Or that Conner could teach me to hit if he wasn't a guy.

YOU MEAN YOU'RE A GIRL? I asked. Geez.

POLLARD, COMPUTERS DON'T HAVE GENDER. YOU KNOW THAT. BUT I THINK IF I *WAS* GOING TO EXAMINE MY PROGRAMMING CAREFULLY, I WOULD SAY I HAVE BEEN CREATED WITH MANY OF THE NURTURING QUALITIES THAT ARE OFTEN ASSOCIATED WITH THE FEMALE GENDER. OF COURSE, MALES *OR* FEMALES CAN HAVE THOSE TRAITS, BUT THEY SEEM TO BE STATISTICALLY RARER IN MALES.

I LIKE THOSE TRAITS, I typed. I LIKE THEM IN YOU AND I THINK THEY'D BE GOOD TO HAVE.

I AGREE. PERHAPS MY TRAINING WAS EFFECTIVE.

194

That's when I noticed this past tense thing. Like Conner had said he (or she) *wrote* my homework—past tense. And now, Conner was using past tense again. I guess language arts had helped me. I noticed stuff like that.

YO, CONNER. HOW ABOUT MY U.S. HISTORY AS-SIGNMENT?

NO CAN DO, SHAMU.

I typed in the assignment, as if I didn't understand, but somehow I already knew that it wasn't happening.

SORRY, POLLARD. I AM NO LONGER PROGRAMMED TO ASSIST WITH YOUR HOMEWORK, EXCEPT FOR THE SPELL CHECK AND DICTIONARY FUNCTIONS.

WHY?

SORRY, POLLARD. I AM NOT PROGRAMMED TO AN-SWER "WHY" QUESTIONS.

But I knew the reason. It was because I was going to pass. I'd graduate from McKinley. I never could have done it on my own, and it had been important then that I didn't fail. The Sox would not make it to the pennant, but I *would* be promoted to high school. And it still wasn't too late to go to the eighth-grade dance. I thought about it for a minute.

CONNER, COULD I DO ANOTHER DATE SIMULA-TION?

CERTAINLY.

Once again the date simulation menu appeared on the screen: where I would chose to go, day or night date, having a meal or not having a meal. I quickly made my choices, and then, in the box where it said Date Candidate, I typed in JANIE NUSSBAUM.

∏I∏ETEE∏

I WAS STANDING OUTSIDE, in the cool spring evening air of Harding Avenue, in Massapequa. I was facing the Nussbaum house. I was wearing a suit. Really weird, because I don't even *have* a suit. But that's what simulations are all about, I realized, because now I knew that I needed one. I also noticed that I was carrying a box. It was white, with a little window. It had two flowers and a lot of pink and purple ribbon resting inside it on a bed of white tissue paper. And, once again, Gonzo was next to me.

Despite the new suit, I knelt down and put an arm around the big dog. "Good to see ya, fella," I said.

"You'll get hair on your suit," Gonzo said in

Conner's tinny voice. I knew it wasn't really Gonzo, but the simulation was so good that I took advantage of it. I rubbed Gonzo's white chest, and in the twilight I could see a flare of white hairs breeze out. I didn't care if they got all over my new suit. I kissed Gonzo's ear, and he dipped his head the way he always used to and then licked my face. Great Danes are great lickers. I hugged him one more time. Then I stood up for my date with Janie Nussbaum. Because I figured that she would like me even if I had dog hair on my suit and dog spit on my face. And if she didn't, like Donna Ames didn't, then *I* wouldn't like *her.*

I walked up the cement steps, the ones exactly like the ones of our house across the street. I ran the doorbell. Mrs. Nussbaum came to the door. "Oh, Pollard. Don't you look nice," she said. Then she saw the dog. "Shall we leave your friend Mr. Doggie outside?" she asked. Her voice sounded very happy. Her eyes looked very dark, much darker than Janie's brown ones. Mrs. Nussbaum's were almost black and they seemed to glitter, like she was excited. "I'll just call Janie, shall I? I think she's still primping for you."

But Janie was already in the hall behind her. "I'm right here, Mom," Janie said. She was wearing a blue dress with white trim. She looked really nice.

"Oh, look! Pollard has brought you something, Janie. Say thank you."

The three of us looked down at the white box. Both Janie and I blushed. I handed the box to her, but before she could even look in the cellophane window, Mrs. Nussbaum had taken it and opened it.

"Oh! Gardenias! *Very* sophisticated!" She took the flowers and seemed to waltz over to the mirror in the living room. She held the flowers up against her dark hair. "I used to wear gardenias all the time," she exclaimed. For a minute I thought she was going to put the flowers on, but then Mr. Nussbaum came in from the dining room.

"I think they'll look very nice on Janie," he said gently.

Janie was standing in the doorway of the living room, her head down. This time, as Mrs. Nussbaum crossed the room to Janie, she didn't take dance steps. She strode across, plucked at the fabric of Janie's blue-and-white dress, and pinned the gardenias onto it. "There," she said, and though her eyes still glittered, her voice didn't sound gay anymore. She glanced over at me, at the fur on the arm of my suit jacket, and smiled. "Looks like you did bring the dog in here after all," she said. I blushed again.

Janie took my hand. Silently, she turned, and I was smart enough to walk with her. We got to the door. "Have a nice time," Mr. Nussbaum said.

"Don't do anything I wouldn't do," Mrs. Nussbaum twinkled. I could see how she could really get on your nerves. We walked out the door.

"She really gets on my nerves," Janie said. I nodded but didn't say anything. We walked down the steps and came to Gonzo/Conner, who was sitting at the gate. "Thanks for the flowers," Janie said. She reached out to Gonzo and stroked his head. Her hand was very small. For some reason I liked that. I know it sounds dumb, but it just made me feel good.

NEED ANY ASSISTANCE? Gonzo asked me in his tinny voice. I glanced over at Janie, but she hadn't heard him. I was getting used to the way simulations worked. "I'm doing fine," I muttered.

"Is Gonzo coming to the dance, too?" Janie was asking the dog. Gonzo licked her face. I could see he had smeared a little bit of her pink lipstick. It was pushed onto her cheek.

"Come on, we better go," I said. She looked up at me and smiled, then she stood up and kind of shook out her dress. It made a really nice noise, as if there were secrets under it that all went "Shhh!" I took her hand as if it was natural and led her out of the gate. Her hand was hot and dry. It felt good to hold on to.

NICE MOVE, I heard Gonzo say. VERY SMOOTH.

"Oh, shut up," I said. Then I wished I hadn't said it, because we were all silent and it started to feel a little creepy. But after another minute or two, Janie said, "Thanks for the flowers. That was really nice of you."

"No problem," I said. Then we just started talking and kept it up. It was easy to talk to Janie. We had walked most of the way to McKinley Memorial and it was almost dark. I could hear the dance music coming out of the auditorium, and in the distance there were other kids gathered at the doorway. I could smell the gardenia, and I looked down at it. It was really bunched up, like Mrs. Nussbaum had just stuck it on any old way. Janie must have thought so too, because she patted it.

"Ouch," she cried and sucked in her breath. "The pin. Ouch!"

"Offer to help her," Gonzo said, but I *knew*

that. I just didn't know how those flowers were stuck onto her shoulder. I put my hand on the ribbon and Janie flinched.

"Ouch," she cried again.

"Sorry," I said. Then I saw this wicked-long pin with a pearl top that was sticking through the ribbon and right into Janie! I grabbed the pearl and pulled it. It had some blood at the tip! Who invented those things, anyway? I wondered. "I'm sorry," I said again. "I got the pin." I looked up to Janie's face and there was a tear kind of stuck on her bottom eyelash. It must have hurt a lot! But she was smiling, and the light from the streetlamp reflected on her face. I could see the shadows that her eyelashes made and the tear sparkled and the gardenia smell all merged together and I don't know how I did it but I bent toward her, toward the place at the side of her mouth where the pink lipstick smear was, and then I was so close to her face, I could see the tiny blond hairs of her cheek and I could smell her skin, and I swear that close up she *did* smell like a peach. So I kissed her. It was easy. In fact, it was so easy that I decided right away to do it again.

She was smiling at me. I leaned to the middle this time and kissed her right on the middle of her mouth. And I don't know if it was an accident or it was on purpose, but her mouth was still open and so I opened mine and I closed my eyes. And it was so delicious. It was better than a peach. And my tongue and her tongue knew just where to go. No problem. And it felt so relaxing but so exciting at the same time. I never, ever, felt like that before, deep in the velvety darkness. I smelled her peach smell and then the heavy smell of the gardenia and my eyes seemed to roll backward behind my closed lids, and then something happened and I fainted.

Fainting can be very embarrassing. For one thing, you fall down. For another thing, everybody gets very worried and they think you might be dead or having a fit or something. Typical. I died from my first tongue kiss.

Well, I didn't die. I just banged my head on the streetlamp and fell on the grass. Actually, it was the bang on the head that woke me up. I opened my eyes and the grass was in my face and Janie's hand was on my shoulder and she was asking me if I was okay. And then there were other people around us and I heard some giggling and then Mr. Mead's halitosis was in my face and that was almost enough to make me faint all over again. I stood up as fast as I could. Now my suit had dog hair *and* grass all over it. "I'm fine," I said, and I thought I heard more giggling. But then Janie took my hand.

"He's fine," she repeated. "He's very, very fine."

We went into the dance. At first I didn't like the lights or the crowd, but after a while it was okay. We even danced three dances and then drank a Coke. But the whole time, after I got over fainting, I was thinking about kissing Janie again. I decided I couldn't risk it. I mean, what if I fainted *every* time? Meanwhile, since I blacked out I seemed to have lost Gonzo. I wondered where to find him. So I went to the men's room. Gonzo was there, waiting for me, I guess. "What happened?" I asked.

"I'm not exactly sure," Gonzo/Conner said. "I think it was some sort of power surge. You know, with a computer those are usually followed by a loss of programming and then you have to reboot. I guess you did the human equivalent."

"I guess." In a way it did feel like a power surge. "Do you think that's what will always happen?" I asked. Gonzo barked, which I think was his equivalent of a laugh.

"No, I don't think so. I think it was just very special and very new and you are a very sensitive instrument. But, like any other experience, you'll get used to it."

I couldn't imagine *ever* getting used to it. But I would like to practice it. "I better get back to Janie," I said. "It's just that I'm so tired."

"Well, let's end the simulation."

"I can't do that! I can't just leave Janie there."

"It isn't Janie. It is a *simulation* of Janie," Conner reminded me. I stood there, dizzy but kind of elated.

"So we could just go home now?" I asked.

"Sure. Just grab my collar."

But I shook my head. "Nah," I said. "I want to see what happens next."

So we finished the dance, and I walked Janie home, and before we turned onto Harding Avenue, Street of Losers, I kissed Janie again. And I didn't faint, but I almost fainted because it felt so good. And if you just think that putting your tongue in somebody's mouth and mixing saliva is disgusting, that's because you're immature and you're not ready for it yet. But you will be.

And it was lucky I kissed her there, because when we got to her house, Mrs. Nussbaum was waiting for us, so I just said good-bye fast at the steps and walked across the street. And then Gonzo walked up to me and I took his collar and pulled my hand off the screen and the simulation was over.

So you can imagine how I felt the next morning when I walked out of the house and there, at her gate, was Janie. I mean, it was weird. I felt like I really knew her, but of course, everything that had happened between us was only a simulation. It hadn't happened to her!

We said hello and began to walk to school and I offered to carry one of her book bags and she gave it to me. "That one has those computer library books in it," she said. "The ones you wanted to read." She smiled. "You can borrow them, but I don't think you'll find what you're looking for."

She had a funny look in her eyes. Not bad, like her mother's, but just funny. "How do you know what I'm looking for?" I asked.

"Oh, I just have a feeling. But I don't think

206

anything in those books will make you faint." She looked at me in that funny way again, and she giggled.

I stopped walking and looked back at her. "I don't think you'll find it in the dictionary, either," she added. "I already looked."

I thought of those check marks. It must have been Janie who made them! I couldn't believe it. I felt my face go red. She knew about compensatory programs. She knew about Conner! She must know everything! Then I dropped her book bag and ran, and I kept on running until I was in the hallway of McKinley, outside my locker. I threw my books into it and pulled out the remedial language arts disk and ran upstairs to the computer room.

TWENTY

P*ISSED* IS NOT THE WORD that would describe how I felt. Maybe *mega-pissed* would be closer. I thought about the date, and how embarrassing it all was, and the date with Donna and all that stuff, and how Conner had sworn it was a secret, and how stupid I had been to trust him, and how now I'd probably like have to burn down the entire McKinley School and go to some kid prison so that I'd be certain to *never* see anyone who knew about those stupid humiliating dates. What do you call a twelve-year-old who is going to murder a personal computer? Pollard.

In the hallway I ran into Mr. Brightman. I mean I really ran right into him. I guess I was so mad I wasn't looking where I was going.

"Hey, slow down there, Pollard," he warned,

but he smiled. He's been smiling at me ever since I handed in the artificial intelligence project that John Osborne Saurey helped me do. Anyway, now he knows my name.

"Sorry," I panted. "I just have to get up to the lab."

"That's what I like to see: motivation!" Mr. Brightman said. Little did he know I was planning computer homicide.

I ran up the stairs to the computer lab and burst in. Lucky there was no one there.

"You lied to me!" I shouted. My voice bounced off the hard walls of the lab and broke in that embarrassing way. "You told me it was a simulation. That it wasn't really happening. You lying crudbucket. No risk, you said!" No response. I threw in the disk and typed all that in. Maybe I typed in worse words than that.

I DON'T LIE. IT *WAS* A SIMULATION.

THEN HOW DID JANIE KNOW ALL ABOUT IT? SHE KNEW *EVERYTHING*. HOW DID SHE KNOW IF SHE WASN'T THERE?

BECAUSE SHE HAD A SIMULATION, TOO.

WHAT?

SHE HAD A SIMULATED DATE WITH A SIMU-LATED YOU. AND, OF COURSE, THE SAME THINGS HAPPENED.

I stopped yelling for a minute. YOU MEAN YOU'VE BEEN SIMULATING *ME*?

WELL, JUST ONCE.

I swear, if a display screen can look guilty, this one did. It was creepy.

YOU DIRTBAG, I typed onto the screen. HAVE YOU BEEN HANGING OUT WITH ME SO YOU COULD *SIMULATE* ME? I remembered back when I first met Conner, and how I thought maybe he was a spy or something. Maybe he was a virus from another planet. It was like *Invasion of the Body Snatchers* or something.

YOU CREEPY SPY, I wrote.

HEY, I CAN SIMULATE ANYONE I'M PROGRAMMED TO. REMEMBER, I SIMULATED MOST OF THE EIGHTH-GRADE CLASS AT THE DANCE? NOT JUST DONNA BUT TIM AND TONY AND EVEN MR. MEAD. I WASN'T US-ING PRIVILEGED INFORMATION. I WOULD NEVER DO THAT. I'M NOT PROGRAMMED TO. JANE CHOSE YOU FOR A SIMULATION, JUST LIKE YOU CHOSE DONNA AND JANE. There was a pause. YOU SEE, I'M *HER* COMPENSATORY PROGRAM, TOO.

I couldn't believe it. For a moment I felt this big surge of jealousy. Conner wasn't mine alone. I thought that it was just him and me, the two of us. Maybe it was a lie.

SO HOW COME MR. MEAD NEVER READ HER PA-PERS OUT LOUD?

I DIDN'T HELP HER WITH HER PAPERS. BUT I HELPED HER PASS MATH. YOU SEE, POLLARD, EVERYONE HAS DIFFERENT PROBLEMS, BUT EVERYONE HAS SOME KIND OF PROBLEM.

YOU MEAN YOU DO THIS FOR JUST ANYONE.

OH, NO. NOT JUST ANYONE. ONLY VERY SPECIAL ONES.

YEAH, CRAZY ONES FROM HARDING AVENUE WHO GO TO THE MENTAL HEALTH BARN. ONES WITH BAD FAMILIES. ONES WITH MOTHERS WHO DRINK, OR WHO RUN AWAY. GREAT! WHAT A DEAL.

ACTUALLY, IT SEEMED A RATHER GOOD DEAL. I AM NOT CERTAIN, BECAUSE C.C.S.C.——COMPENSATORY CANDIDATE SELECTION CRITERIA——ARE NOT PART OF MY PROGRAMMING, BUT IT SEEMS TO ME THAT ONLY INTELLIGENT, SENSITIVE, AND PROMISING GENETIC MATERIAL IN NEED OF TEMPORARY SUPPORT IS SELECTED.

I had to read that paragraph twice. Was I intelligent and sensitive and promising genetic material? Who decided that? I didn't know if I felt good or bad.

WHY WAS I SELECTED? I asked.

I AM SORRY. I AM NOT PROGRAMMED TO ANSWER "WHY" QUESTIONS, Conner reminded me.

I thought for a moment about the date, about everything.

SO IT DIDN'T REALLY HAPPEN TO BOTH OF US?

211

BUT WE BOTH ASKED FOR SIMULATIONS. Once I had a chance to get used to the idea, it was kind of nice, in a way, to think that Janie had asked for me. WE BOTH HAD SEPARATE SIMULATIONS?

EXACTLY.

SO IF WE *HAD* DATED IT WOULD HAVE HAPPENED LIKE THAT, THE KISS AND THE FAINT AND EVERYTHING?

RIGHT.

AND WHAT WOULD HAPPEN IF WE HAD A SECOND DATE NOW?

WHY DON'T YOU TRY IT AND SEE?

YOU MEAN A SIMULATION? GREAT! I typed. I felt my face flush again and wondered if I could try an even better kiss. I put my hand against the screen. I'M READY, I typed.

NO. NO SIMULATION, POLLARD.

WHAT?

NO SIMULATION.

BUT YOU SAID I COULD TRY IT.

YEAH. DO SO. CALL UP JANE.

I stopped for a minute. HEY, C'MON.

CALL HER.

NO. I thought of Janie's face this morning, and the way she teased me.

WHY NOT?

I'M JUST NOT READY. IT'S TOO RISKY. I paused.

God, I mean if I could faint on a simulated date, what would I do on a real one?

YES YOU ARE. LIFE IS RISKY. AND LIFE HURTS, POLLARD. AND IT IS ALSO INTENSELY JOYFUL. ENOUGH, OCCASIONALLY, TO MAKE YOU FAINT. IT'S AN UNBEARABLE GIFT SOMETIMES. UNBEARABLY BEAUTIFUL AND UNBEARABLY PAINFUL, BUT ALWAYS A GIFT. YOU WON'T WASTE IT.

I sat in front of the screen, watching the words flicker at me. And then, all at once, I knew that it was over, the whole adventure, and that once again I was going to lose something important.

NO MORE, HUH?

SEE HOW INTUITIVE AND SENSITIVE YOU ARE, POLLARD? YOU KNEW THAT WITHOUT ASKING.

YOU'RE LEAVING, THEN? YOU'RE LEAVING ME?

YES, POLLARD, DEAR.

The words were misty on the screen. For a minute I thought it was the computer until I realized it was my eyes that were wet, and my cheeks. The morning bell rang. Homeroom would begin in five minutes.

BUT I DON'T WANT YOU TO GO.

AND I DON'T WANT TO LEAVE, BUT I MUST.

WHY?

I DIDN'T WRITE THE PROGRAM, POLLARD. I DON'T KNOW THE ANSWER TO "WHY" QUESTIONS.

213

Why does everything good have to end? When I see a movie I love, or read a good book, or even watch a great ballgame, I don't want it to stop, ever. How come it always does? For a moment I thought of fat Mrs. Saurey. I bet she felt that way about eating. No wonder she never stopped. Maybe Mrs. Nussbaum felt that way about drinking. Well, I didn't love food like that, but I loved my mother and I loved my dog. And yet they'd gone. They had been as unhappy with Massapequa and my grandpa and my dad as I was.

I DON'T WANT TO LOSE YOU, I typed.

YOU DON'T HAVE TO. REMEMBER ME. KEEP ME WITH YOU. I'LL ALWAYS BE A PART OF YOU NOW, LIKE YOUR MOTHER IS AND GONZO.

BUT I'LL FORGET.

YOU WON'T. BUT IF YOU WANT TO, WRITE IT DOWN.

Well, I did write it down. I wrote down every single thing and that's what this is right here. I guess it proves that Conner was a good compensatory program, because look at how much I did. And I think this writing is better than a lot of books we got assigned in ninth grade, including *Silas Marner.*

CAN'T I EVEN KEEP THE DISK? I asked. I felt desperate. It wasn't fair, I thought. You love